THE SUITCASE OF SECRETS

THE SUITCASE OF SECRETS

Connie Hannah

I would like to thank Victoria, Kai, Mandy, Jeff, and family and friends for all of their encouragement, positive thoughts, and for giving me the strength I needed to write this book. I love you all.

CHAPTER ONE

The time has come to open the suitcase of my life. It has been years since I've unpacked the memories, celebrations and secrets that make me the person I am today. When I first thought of unpacking everything, I wasn't sure if I had the courage to do it. After many hours of prayer, I now have the courage to face my fears. I have indeed come a long way. There have been numerous triumphs and so many moments of joy despite the setbacks. I have reached the point in my life that in order for me to continue onward, I must acknowledge and let go of the past. I am ready to return for the first and last time into the often dark and winding path of my past no matter how painful or scary it may appear.

I sat down on the floral carpet in my bedroom in the home I share with my husband and two children. It is a sunny day outside, but there is a slight cool breeze blowing into my bedroom windows causing the curtains to billow in and out. I have opened the windows so that the fresh, clean fall air can surround me. I can hear the birds in the trees in our front yard singing a song of peace and happiness. I think if I were a bird, I would be singing that same song today. The house is extremely quiet. The kids are at their grandparent's house for the weekend and my husband is on a trip. I think this is the perfect weekend to open my leather suitcase of memories. It is deep brown in color with brass trim and numerous torn and broken straps. It houses many items that I rarely use, but is kept close by my side just in case I am hit with a mood of nostalgia

Trying to hold back tears, I cautiously peek in the main compartment and slowly begin removing its contents one by one. I taste the salty tears rolling down my cheeks and into my mouth. I breathe deeply and get myself composed for the task ahead. Knowing what I must do, I slowly put my hands into the bottom of the suitcase and work my way to the top.

As I push things around to get to the bottom of the case, a precious pink flocked dress with a lace crinoline appears. Lying beside the dress is a pair of black patent leather shoes and a pair of yellowed gloves that were once white.

During my early childhood, up until I was about four years old, my momma, brother and I lived in a small, white clapboard house in the City of Atlanta. Our little white house sat at the corner of Charles Allen Drive and Highland Avenue. The streets were lined with small, wooden two and three bedroom houses with screened porches and uneven sidewalks. Huge oak and maple trees towered over the sidewalks and streets. Momma liked this street because it had a playground at the end of it and all the kids would play together in the evening while the moms and dads sat on their front porches and talked. Our street was so pretty and looked as if it taken directly off the front page of *The Saturday Evening Post* newspaper. Everyone who lived on our street knew and looked out for their neighbors. I remember it was a hot, steamy, summer afternoon when Momma got home from her job downtown and noticed that we had a new neighbor. Momma asked our next door neighbor, Charlie, who Momma said was a "sometimes" house painter but seemed to spend more time at home than working, what was our new neighbors name. Charlie told us that his name was Jay Blackwood. Mr. Jay had recently moved into the other side of the duplex where Charlie lived. Mr. Jay a tall, olive skinned fella who seemed to be very friendly, and was always smiling.

The next day, Mr. Jay came walking down the sidewalk from his house just about the time Momma parked her beaten up Green Ford Falcon station wagon along the street in front of our house. This became a daily routine and they were always smiling at each other and talking a lot. I really liked him a whole lot. When he came over to sit and talk with my momma, he would bring me and my brother a box of Boston Baked Beans candy and sometimes a giant swirled sucker with lots of colors on it. He liked to throw the ball to the kids on the playground in the evenings and make us laugh. I asked Momma where Mr. Jay worked and she told me that he was an electrician. He made the lights turn on and off. Before that, he lived on a ship out in the ocean. I told Momma that it seemed like Mr. Jay had a fun life. She laughed at me and said that she thought that too.

As the months went by, Mr. Jay spent more time at our house. He came and ate dinner almost every night. Momma was always smiling and singing when Mr. Jay came around. About a year after Mr. Jay entered our lives, he and Momma started talking about a wedding. Soon, my brother Kris and I would have a new daddy along with new aunts, uncles and cousins.

One Sunday afternoon after church, Kris and I rode in Mr. Jay's fancy red car with bat wings, to Carroll County, Georgia for the first time. We were on our way to meet our new relatives, Aunt Sara and Uncle Allen. I was so excited that my little family was becoming a big family, and this was indeed the coolest thing in the whole wide world. It was a week later, after we had met our new relatives, Mr. Jay bought Kris and I brand new clothes for the wedding from the big Sears store on Ponce DeLeon Avenue. The ceremony was at Aunt Sara and Uncle Allen's house. After the ceremony, Kris and I stayed with my cousins while my mamma and Mr. Jay went on their honeymoon (whatever that was).

Just before the wedding started, I decided to take a comb and a pair of scissors under the table, that the wedding cake sat on, and gave myself a brand new haircut. I then made my grand entrance out from under the table to show off my new hairdo. I remember everyone looking at me and laughing. When my momma retold this story years later, I learned that I had cut my bangs to the very top of my forehead.

Mr. Jay looked down at me and wasn't happy with my new haircut. He got very angry with me and started yelling. His face became red and purple and the veins in his neck were poking out. I started to cry and became scared. I was frightened and did not like the wicked look on his face. He had a glare in his eyes that seemed to look right past me. My momma went over and talked with Mr. Jay and he eventually calmed down. Momma then came over to me and told me that this day was not about me and I better get it together fast. She told me this was her special day and I was not going to ruin it for her. I said, "Yes mam."

I walked to the side of the table where the cake was sitting and stood there and pouted. My momma and Mr. Jay stood in front of a preacher and he talked about love and stuff and then they kissed, yuck. Another man came over to where we all were standing and started taking pictures. It turned out to be festive day and Momma was really proud to be married to Mr. Jay. It was a fun day for me and my brother. Aunt Sara let us eat as much cake as we wanted and later that day, we all sat in the family room and watched *Chitty Chitty Bang Bang*, I liked staying at my Aunt Sara's house.

After Momma and Mr. Jay got back from their honeymoon, she came into my bedroom early one Saturday morning and announced that we were going shopping at the big Sears store where we got our clothes for the wedding. I was so excited because we were going to the big, fancy store with all the pretty clothes.

Before Mr. Jay came into our lives, we didn't shop at Sears or any other big department stores. Most of my cotton mu-mu dresses with ties on the shoulders were homemade. Although my clothes were always clean and pressed, I envied the girls at my school with frilly dresses and fancy socks and shoes. But today, my momma and I were going to the big store to get another special dress for another special day, or at least that was what Mr. Jay told me.

While riding up the escalator at the Sears store, I asked Momma why we were shopping for more outfits and what was the special day that Mr. Jay was talking about? Momma, beaming with happiness, looked down at me and had a large smile on her face. She told me that on Friday morning, Kris and I were going to be adopted by Mr. Jay and we needed to look nice when we went and talked to the Judge. I really did not understand most of what Momma was talking about, but I did go around my kindergarten class telling everyone that I was going to be "bydopted." It really did not matter that much to me though. What really mattered was that I was getting a new dress and a new daddy.

As I look back and remember the day of the adoption, I see several pictures in my mind. Some recollections were of my momma not having to struggle and always being so sad and worried about money. Maybe now we could go on a vacation to the ocean, or go to the movies. If my momma and daddy (Mr. Jay) made a lot of money, we may be able to go out and eat at McDonald's. The list just went on and on. Even though my "new dad" got mad a lot, and his face turned red and purple, maybe life being so much easier on my momma would make the good outweigh the bad.

CHAPTER TWO

Laying the pink dress on my bed, I continued to unpack the mountain of belongings that now seems to be exploding out of the opened suitcase.

With the unpacking underway, the series of events in my life that took place years ago are so vivid and crystal clear as if they happened just yesterday. All of the anger, confusion and fear I locked away forty four years ago is coming to the surface. The things I never dared to talk about openly are being exposed. I am going to have to do my best to muddle through these memories from so long ago. I know that it will be life changing to reveal these secrets of the past, but it also frightens me that people will look at me differently. That some will somehow believe that I brought these things upon myself. Now realistically speaking, I know that this is an irrational feeling, but on a human level, guilt and regret go hand and hand with physical, sexual, and emotional abuse. The abuser is a master at convincing the victim that they are to blame and that the reasons for the abuse are their fault. So I will ask my readers to bear with me as I slowly work through the details of the remaining chapters.

I am, by dredging up all these old feeling, fears, heartaches, and triumphs, coming to a very clear realization that one cannot begin to fill their suitcase with new memories until they have completely emptied and acknowledged the one.

The next item I reach for from the suitcase is the birth announcement for my younger sister Katie. She was born 2 years after my mom and Mr. Jay, who I began calling dad, were married. I was 6 years old when I overheard Momma on the phone telling my grandparents that she was pregnant. I had a sneaky feeling that she thought that by having my dad's biological child, that maybe, this would chill him out some. Hopefully, he would direct his attention to his new baby and away from me and my brother.

In the fall of 1968, along with all the excitement of a new baby, there was also the move from our home on Charles Allen Road in the Virginia Highlands' area of Atlanta, to East Point. Our new home was a small brick ranch with three bedrooms and a big family room. Since my dad was retired Navy, they were able to purchase their first home with a VA loan. The home costs about $12,000.00 which was considered a lot of money at that time. We had a small cement front porch with three brick stairs leading up to the front door. There was a two-car carport, a small side yard, and a huge fenced back yard. Next door to us, on the left side of our home was where the Henshaws lived and they had one daughter named Betty. Betty was a couple of years older than me and very gangly. She had metal braces, and big green, rectangular glasses. We did not play together very much since she was older and a bit more mature.

On the right side of our home were the Dudaks. They had a son named Derrick. I felt bad for Derrick too. My friends and I who lived on my street used to pour everything we could find (mustard, ketchup, hot sauce, grape juice, etc.) into a coke bottle and tell him it was "magic juice." He drank it every time until one day he got so sick that he threw up all evening. His mom asked him had he eaten something bad and he told her about the magic juice. After I got a spanking with the bolo paddle and yelled at by my mom, that was pretty much the end of our concoction.

At first glance we looked like the average middle class family. However, beyond the curtains of our East Point home, life was anything but ordinary. My mom, brother and I spent our days walking on egg shells. With each day, it seemed to get worse for us.

Unfortunately, for the three of us, this pregnancy was the start of the vicious and violent behavior that would be displayed by my dad towards Momma and eventually it would trickle down to my brother and me. We had a few glimpses of his temper and cruelty up to this point with screaming fits and brutal spankings, but these episodes were becoming more intense.

As I looked at the birth announcement letting the world know that my sweet baby sister Katie was born I felt tears stinging my eyes. I began to think back on the days of my momma's pregnancy and how frightened she must have been.

I have asked myself a million times how did my momma survive that pregnancy and carry my sister almost to full term. This will always be a mystery to me. She not only continued to work, but she also raised my brother and I. My brave Momma did everything within her power to keep herself and her children from being hurt either emotionally or physically by the man that she had once seen as her hero. I think she truly began to believe that heroes are only found in movies and other people's lives, and realized that her new husband was not by any means, a hero. He was a sick man who was filled with hate and this profound hate would spill over into our lives for years to come.

The hidden secrets of my family will begin to surface in this chapter but no one in the outside world had a clue. In order to keep these secrets under lock and key we had to not only try and survive while we were at home, but we also had to work that much harder at pretending that our lives were perfect while in public. How we pulled this off I will never know, but boy were we convincing. I think at times we even fooled ourselves into believing this fairy tale family, that we portrayed, was real.

In the summer of 1969, my childhood days on Connolly Drive were filled with fun. My best buddies were Carey and Jillian who lived across the street. Their parents, Mr. and Mrs. Evans, were good friends with my parents. We were more like family rather than neighbors. We all ate dinner together several nights during the week and all of us were pretty inseparable. The Evans also had an older son Mike, who hung out with my brother. There were many boys in the neighborhood that gathered and played touch football on our front lawn. When not playing football, Kris and Mike hid in the bushes and bombed my Barbie house with their G.I. Joe army men. Carey, Jillian and myself screamed for Helen, our maid, to make them stop destroying our dollhouses that we had spent hours setting up. Each time, after Helen threatened them with having to come inside, the terror would stop. We would then stay under the carport for hours on end playing with our Barbie dolls and laughing. These were such good times.

The good time usually lasted until about 5:00 in the evenings on the weekdays. Then "he" got home. If it was a bad day at work, our fun filled days often ended with a night of terror. One summer evening, after such a great day playing with my friends, I sat at a small red table in my bedroom drawing and coloring. It was very quiet in the house until the carport door slammed announcing his arrival. I could hear his voice getting louder and louder. My mom, who was in the kitchen cooking dinner, began crying very loudly. A familiar blanket of fear enveloped me. This was not going to be a good night for any of us. "Whose baby is this because I know it's not mine!" He kept asking Momma over and over again. Each time, his voice got louder and louder. "Who are you sleeping with at your office?" He demanded. "I know you have been sleeping around because you are nothing but a slut!"

I listened to the yelling and a wave of nausea swept through my stomach. I wanted to run into the kitchen to protect my momma, but I was too scared. From previous experience, I knew that any intervention would make him angrier and I would pay dearly. Instead of going into the kitchen I walked to my bedroom and put a pillow over my head attempting to drown out the screaming. About Thirty minutes later the yelling and crying abruptly stopped. We were called to the table for dinner and everyone sat in their usual place. My brother and sister sat at the back of the oval table. Me and dad sat at the ends of the table with Momma on the outside so that she could get anything my dad might need. As we all sat there that evening in complete silence, my dad laughed loudly. He then wanted to know why we were all so quiet. He looked at all three of us and told us that we needed to learn to "toughen up." We kept our silence. It was almost with our silence that we were each praying that the yelling had ended for the evening.

The next morning was Sunday and we all woke up to the sounds of the Gospel Jubilee playing loudly on the television. One of the most popular shows in the South, Gospel Jubilee featured gospel quartets that sang Baptist church hymns. This was a ritual in our home every week. Dad sang and whistled. Momma got up and fixed a big Sunday morning breakfast of scrambled cheddar cheese eggs, grits, bacon and homemade biscuits with jelly or sorghum syrup.

After breakfast, we all finished getting ready and then loaded up in my mom's Oldsmobile Sedan and headed to Headland Heights Baptist Church. We went to our Sunday school classes dressed up and perfectly polished. Our Sunday faces were in perfect place and all of us were on our best behavior. We sang and worshiped in the church service like all the other families. At the end of the sermon, my dad would go down and kneel at the altar. He would cry and pray. Watching him do this, week after week, made my skin crawl. It was all an act.

I was sitting quietly watching this cruel and evil man doing everything in his power to convince the world that he should win the grand prize for the "Christian father of the year." I could not believe what I was seeing. Where was this kind, loving man every other day, hour or minute of the week?

How could he get down on his knees and put on such a show and then go home and physically batter his family? Why couldn't we just get a little bit of that person when he came home from work? I could not justify this in my mind and certainly did not understand his behavior.

Despite my dads praying and crying, it didn't make things better at home. He progressively started acting more bizarre and his explosions began to occur more frequently.

It was around 7:30am on June 11, 1969, I woke up and put on my peter pan collared shirt, plaid shorts and pink keds. I was excited because today was the 3rd day of Vacation Bible School at my church. I loved going to VBS because I got to get away from my reality. I was surrounded by sweet, kind and encouraging people. They didn't tell me that I was "useless and ugly" at VBS. I was told that I was loved and I was a precious child of God. At VBS, I felt good about myself and felt safe. Eating sugar cookies and drinking grape juice as a morning snack rounded out the magic of that sacred place.

After getting dressed and ready for bible school, I headed to the kitchen to see what Momma had fixed for breakfast. Instead of my momma, I found our family friend, Miss Shelly, preparing eggs and biscuits for my brother and myself. I asked her where my momma was and she said "didn't you hear the ambulance outside of your bedroom window last night? Your baby sister was born early this morning."

All of this did not register at the moment, and all I could think of was if I was going to be able to go to VBS today. When I asked if we were going, Miss Shelly told me that we would not be able to go today.

This news was just devastating to me. My safe and sacred haven had been taken away from me just because my stupid sister was born. I thought it was so unfair and I ran to my bedroom and cried. In between the tears, I heard Miss Shelly talking on the phone to my grandparents.

I walked to my bedroom door and stuck my ear out as far as I could. She told them that my momma was doing fine now but there had been some major complications. Apparently, Momma and my new baby sister came very close to not making it once they reached the hospital. My momma's water broke and then she was bleeding uncontrollably. The paramedics came in an ambulance and did everything they could to stop the bleeding but she had lost so much blood that things were looking pretty grim. As they arrived at Georgia Baptist Hospital, Dr. Baxter, Momma's doctor, came out and told my dad that there has been so much blood lost, it did not look like my momma and sister would pull through. He assured my dad that he would do everything in his power to save them.

Several minutes passed, which I am sure seemed like hours, Dr. Baxter came back from the double doors and told my dad that my momma and Katie had made it to this point and the next 24 hours would be critical. My dad thanked the doctor. He put on a show in the waiting room that could have possibly won him an Academy Award. He did all the things a caring and loving husband should do. All of the folks in the waiting room consoled him and told him how lucky his family was to have him. Once again, he fooled everyone and played the grieving martyr like a pro. He failed to mention that the previous week; he was accusing his wife of being a slut and having another man's baby. Wow, the things that slip our memories.

After about a week in the hospital, Momma and Katie were released and came home. I was so excited they were home and I could now hold and play with my new little sissy. For several weeks, life in our home was pleasant. Folks from our church came and brought casseroles, macaroni and cheese, cakes and pies. It felt good to be able to laugh and play without fear of the unknown shadowing over me.

My momma was resting in her bed and trying to regain her strength after she came home from the hospital. She was talking in a whispered voice, but I could still overhear her talking to Miss Shelly. Momma told Miss Shelly what happened the evening her water broke. She said that she was in her sewing room working on some baby clothes when Jay stormed in and began asking her again "whose baby this was?" She said she had gotten so tired of his accusations of her sleeping around. She told him he knew this baby was his. He told her that she was a liar because he had a vasectomy several years ago and there was no way this baby could be his. Momma knew he had not had a vasectomy and that she certainly had not been with any other man.

As she stood up and started to walk out of the room, he charged towards her, got in her face and told her that he was not going to take care of a "bastard child." As she tried to get around him, she started feeling pain in her lower abdomen and told him she was hurting. He started laughing and continued blocking her access to the door. She walked from side to side trying to get out of the room while he was determined to taunt her and keep her under his control. He continued to torture her and tried to force her to say that the baby belonged to another man.

As the situation became more intense, my momma felt an enormous stabbing pain in her abdomen. When she looked down, knowing that her water had broken, she noticed blood was running down her legs and her pain was getting increasingly sharper. She yelled for my dad to call for an ambulance. She proceeded to lie down on the floor, propping her feet up and prayed that help with come soon.

While Momma was waiting for medical help, my dad kept telling her that she was being punished for having another man's baby and this was just God's way of getting even with her. She tried as hard as she could to tune him out and focus on bringing this baby safely into the world.

Minutes later, the paramedics entered the house and started an IV. They worked as hard as they could to get her stable and to the hospital. Once at the hospital, the medical team got Momma and Katie stabilized and a miracle occurred. My mom and baby sister survived even through the torment that had taken place earlier that evening.

Miss Shelly listened to her account of the details of that night, but I don't think she really believed that my dad could have been that cold and cruel. This was a man who was a deacon of the church. He was always talking about his family and how much he loved them. Miss Shelley recalled a conversation with dad a couple of months ago. He told her he would die for his family. We were the only thing that mattered in his life except for his love for God. Miss Shelley told Momma how blessed she was to have such a good man for a husband and she should remember that. She also told Momma how relieved she was that she and the baby made it and hopefully having a new baby in the house would help to make things a bit calmer.

As she listened to the words that Miss Shelly had spoken, Momma came to the conclusion that Miss Shelly did not really believe all the things she had told her about my dad. She figured Momma was probably a bit loopy from all of the medication and was not clear on the events that led up to Katie's birth. I mean, how could anyone look at this loving, sweet, and dedicated family man and think that he could, in any way, be cruel or hurt anybody. You could just see the loving way he looked at his family and knew that he would never harm a hair on their heads. After Miss Shelly made these comments, Momma realized that she and her children had done a great job of convincing people that our home life was to be envied.

After this horrible experience and after hearing nothing but compliments and admiration for this strong, supportive, Christian man, our family felt that we had no other choice but to keep up the facade that we had created. The sad thing about all of this was that the more we perfected our acting, the worse things got at home.

I remember being that terrified little girl sitting in her room wondering why nobody would help me get away from the "monster." In the movies, there was always someone who seemed to save the day. Why didn't somebody come and save me?

CHAPTER THREE

After the memory of my momma and Katie almost dying, I am going to have to make myself dig deep into this suitcase no matter how hard it is. I know that I cannot heal and move on with my life without facing these demons and it is time once and for all.

Hesitantly reaching in, the next item I remove is a man's watch. This watch is a reminder of a night that I will probably never completely erase from my mind and sometimes reoccurs in the form of a nightmare. When this nightmare haunts me, I just lie in my bed and keep telling myself "he cannot hurt you again." But, it is much easier to tell myself that than to truly believe it deep within. This chapter will definitely evoke feelings of sadness and will make you want to give that scared little girl a very big hug.

As my family grew from three to four and the City of Atlanta school system became more integrated, my parents decided that it was time to move out to the country. In 1973, after living in the city for 10 years, our family moved to a small country town and into a traditional brick ranch house in Douglas County.

The move was a huge transition for my brother and me. We were city kids. The fast paced energy of the city was all we had known and now we were out in a small country town where the main social outlet was church. A small town where the kids at school wore black rock n' roll t-shirts and Converse high tops, while I was walking around with my pink corduroy pants, peter pan collared shirts, and black and white saddle shoes. I looked and felt like a fish out of water.

I started the fourth grade at Beulah Elementary School. It was a small brick and steel building only a few blocks from our new home. My teachers' first name was also her last name, Kathy Cathy. I thought that was so funny. After being in Ms. Cathy's class for several months, I decided she was the coolest teacher ever and maybe things were not going to be so bad after all. Ms. Cathy embraced me and took me under her wing. I don't know if she had a sense that my home life was not as I had portrayed or if she just saw a spark in this tiny little red head's eye. Whatever she saw, was just what I needed to make me feel a part of something, and I liked it.

As the months went by, I slowly began to make new friends at school and church. Although there were many new things in my life that were positive, there were a lot of things that had not changed. For our entire family, starting over in a new town was the beginning of having to perfect our act again. We would once again have to convince those around us that we were a close knit, loving, fine Christian family. The secret had to be guarded with all our might. We had to keep "him" protected for the safety of us all. So, I continued to cry all night and put on a smile all day. It was the only life I knew. I somehow made it through the fourth grade and was now a fifth grader at Beulah Elementary. It was a Friday night in early winter and my mom and dad had gone to the local drug store to pick up a prescription. My brother, sister and I were left at home while they were gone. The three of us were watching *The Brady Bunch,* and just hanging out. When our parents returned home, my dad asked me if I had seen his watch. I did not think much about the question and answered with a simple "no." He asked me if I was sure and wanted to know if I had done something with his watch. Although I gave the same answer, he continued to drill me and I was getting increasingly annoyed. I felt as if I was being interrogated. After ten or so minutes, the questioning ended and dad went down to his shop in the basement.

Not long after that, it was my bedtime. I brushed my teeth, got my glass of water, and kissed Momma goodnight. I was fast asleep in no time at all. I don't know how late it was when someone stormed into my bedroom, grabbed me by my arm and jerked me out of the bed. Startled from a deep sleep, it wasn't until I was being beaten on my legs and back that I realized that it was my dad. He was yelling furiously, "You put my watch behind the toaster! You hid my watch and you lied to me you good for nothing loser!"

Paralyzed with terror, I remember wetting all over myself as I was being hit. I pleaded for him to stop. It was so scary and I can still remember the fear and the utter panic I experienced after being yanked out of a deep sleep and hit over and over again while yelling "Stop daddy stop. You are hurting me, please..."

I could hear Momma in her bedroom across the hall sobbing as my beating continued. She came across the narrow hallway into my room a few minutes after my dad left. She hugged me tightly and rocked me as I began to calm down. All the while, saying "I am sorry, I am so sorry. I do not know what to do; if we leave he will find us and hurt us. Please forgive me." Like we had done many times before, we cried together. It was so very clear that neither she nor I knew how to make the terror stop. She changed the sheets on my bed and helped me to get cleaned up. All the while, she just kept telling me that she was so sorry. How could we keep him from getting angry so often and taking his anger out on the three of us. We found ourselves, as the old cliché goes "walking on egg shells" each and every day hoping that we did not crack or break the shell. If we did, there would be hell to pay.

The next morning, my dad was sitting at the breakfast table. He glared at me intensely and asked me if I knew why he had gotten so angry last night. I told him that I did not but kept my response to those few words. He said that when he asked me earlier if I had seen his watch that I had lied to him. He was determined that I had hidden his stupid watch behind the toaster in the kitchen. I knew I had not lied but I also knew better than to protest. He proceeded to tell me that he thought I was a sneaky liar and a thief and "nothing amounts to nothing." I sat there quietly and listened without uttering a single word.

I was confused as to why he would think that I had hidden his watch. The more I thought about it, I remembered seeing my dad washing the supper dishes the night before and putting his Timex watch on the kitchen window sill. I suspected that the watch got knocked off and fell behind the toaster. Why would he think that I did something with it?

It seemed that lately, he was accusing all of us of doing some pretty crazy stuff. Was he just tired from work or was it something more? I was not sure but his behavior was getting more and more bizarre by the day.

CHAPTER FOUR

The next item I retrieve from the suitcase is an old, faded black and white photo of my brother and me. In the picture Kris looked to be about 6 years old and I was about 3. It was taken before the sadness and terror invaded our lives. In the photograph, Kris is wearing Fruit of the Loom white undies, a t-shirt and a fireman's helmet. I am wearing pinkish undies, a short gown, and I am pushing my favorite baby doll in her baby stroller.

This was the last time I remember my brother and I being truly happy as kids. I have sadly not seen my brother in over ten years, but the next chapter will focus on his drug use, his arrest and basically the downfall of a boy who could have been whatever he wanted to be. If only he had been nurtured, cherished, treated with respect and loved by his dad. This is Kris' story...

Kris was born on December 19th, 1959. I don't really know the details of his birth since I was not yet born. From what I know from my momma, Kris's early childhood years were some of the most painful for her. She has never shared any details with me and perhaps never will. Growing up, my brother was a genius that could pretty much figure anything out. He was good at taking things apart and putting them back together. Really, he was just plain ol' brilliant.

There are several really horrifying memories I have of the emotional and physical abuse that was taken out on my brother but one sticks with me and has for many years. This night has haunted me and I can still recall my brother's fear as this horrendous nightmare took place.

Up until about high school, my brother was a great student. He played a couple of sports and although athletic, he was still fairly quiet and was equally interested in writing, drawing and pretty much anything that was creative or artistic.

During the fall of tenth grade, my brother began to change. As the first few months of school passed by Kris seemed to become less and less interested in studying and applying himself in the classroom. His grades were not nearly as good as they had been in the past, but everyone thought that it was just the teen thing and his hormones were taking over temporarily.

Kris began to hang around some new friends and did not see many of his old church buddies. He did not want to study when he got home from school and wanted to stay in his room, which was in the finished portion of the basement. He started listening to some pretty "wild" music like Mott the Hoople, Alice Cooper and Black Sabbath. He would come home from school, go straight to his room. He usually would not come out until Momma called him up for supper. At suppertime, he would sit quietly at the table and not really engage in conversation with the family. I could see that he was slowly detaching himself at school and at home. As the school year progressed, Kris was basically becoming someone I did not recognize. It was a beautiful spring evening in April and our family had just finished eating dinner. My dad went out to our back yard to work on getting his small vegetable garden ready to plant this summer. Momma, Katie and I were sitting at the kitchen table talking and getting caught up from the week and making plans for our weekend. It was a peaceful evening so far and everyone seemed to be in good moods, even dad. Such evenings were always a welcomed relief. Although we knew it was fleeting, my mother, brother, Katie and I felt safe and we lived in gratitude on such evenings.

Thankful for the break between dad's violent rages, we were winding down and hoping the remainder of the night would pass without incident. Our peace ended around 9:00

pm. Katie and I were getting ready for bed when we heard my dad beating his fist on my brothers' bedroom door. He was yelling for him to open the door.

Momma heard a commotion and she went to the door that leads down the basement stairs to Kris' bedroom. She knelt down and prayed that my dad would not harm him. I went and sat by her side as dad managed to break down my brother's bedroom door. Suddenly, my dad began screaming as loudly as he could and all I could hear was my brother hollering "no, no, no." We could hear my dad's fist hitting Kris over and over and over. I could still hear my brother begging and pleading for him to stop, but the violent beating continued. The fear and pain in my brother's voice echoed up those stairs for what seemed to be forever. My brother was whaling and crying so hard that he was literally gasping for air. My momma and I sat with our arms around each other, silently praying that he would not kill Kris in his fit of anger. My dad stomped up the stairs and when he got to the top, he just looked at me and Momma, and with an evil expression and started laughing. He asked us why we were so upset. He just continued to laugh and taunt us for his own pleasure. Dad then ordered me and Momma to the kitchen where he proceeded to lock the door so we could not leave. He instructed us that if we tried to leave the house, we would not make it out of the driveway alive. Momma and I sat on the kitchen floor and wondered if tonight would be the night he took our lives. As we sat motionless, he paced back and forth in front of the door and laughed loudly as he told us that "we looked like a couple of pathetic pigs rooting on his kitchen floor."

After about six hours or so after being held hostage, my dad looked at me and told me that I better go and get in that bed or I would be next. I ran to my bedroom, cracked the door, turned off the light and climbed into my bed pulling the sheets tightly over my head. I concentrated hard on detaching from that place and pretended that I was at the ocean watching the wave's crash and the seagulls soar above me. I eventually calmed myself and dozed off to sleep. For weeks to come, every time I would close my eyes at night, I could hear my brother crying, and begging for help and there was nothing I could do for him. Echoing sounds coming up those stairs will haunt me forever. I wanted so badly to help him, but knew I could not. I was totally hopeless and helpless. The next morning, we all got up and came to the breakfast table to eat before getting ready to head to Aunt Sara's for the day. Despite my brother's brutal beating last night, we were all excited about the fun filled day ahead that would include a picnic and water skiing. I tried hard not to stare at Kris's bruised face. I thought he looked pretty good after such a violent beating.

As we arrived at the lake, I could see my cousins were already in the boat skiing. We took our picnic stuff out of our car and put it on a cement picnic table beside the water. We could not wait to get in that cool, refreshing water and splash around as all kids love to do. I looked over at my brother, and as he took his shirt off, I quickly realized why his face was not extremely bruised. His back was black and blue. He had cuts and abrasions all over upper and lower back. I felt sick as I walked away from him towards the boat. No one said a word the whole day about Kris' injuries. There were no questions. By now, I was a professional at pretending, so I just played and acted as if life was good. On the inside, my heart hurt so badly for my brother.

Several days after my dad beat my brother, I asked my momma what had set him off. Sometimes there was a reason, other times there were none. My mom told me that when my dad went downstairs, he smelled a funny odor coming from under my brothers' door. When he asked him to open the door, he heard Kris shuffling around in his room and opening his window. After busting down the door, dad found my brother had been smoking pot.

Whether we were right or wrong, the severity of our punishment was always extreme. Even in this instance of Kris' drug use, it seems my dad had damaged Kris's soul and spirit beyond repair.

Kris had a gentle spirit and could not handle the ongoing abuse, beatings, and terrorizing of himself and those he loved. He had finally given up. This was the beginning of the end of the brother I had known. I will share a couple of really sad stories from Kris' tormented soul in the next few chapters. I miss you brother.

CHAPTER FIVE

I am going to have to take a small break from the unpacking so that I can go and get some Kleenex and wipe my eyes. Hearing the echoes of Kris begging for his life is just too much for me to digest. There are several memories that I am dredging up that I thought had been put away forever. Reliving these memories is overwhelming, yet necessary.

Okay, the tears are dried and I am ready to reach back in and continue this mission. I root around and pull out what appears to be a letter from the Police Chief of Smyrna. What a jerk!

As life moved painfully along, I graduated from high school in 1980 with a high GPA and a low self esteem. As I reviewed my options for college, my main desire was to get as far away from this place as I could. When looking at schools, however, I knew that I would have to apply to in-state schools since my parents were not helping with any tuition or room and board expenses. I decided to apply, and was accepted to Valdosta State College in South Georgia. It was 5 hours from home and close to the beach. It was just perfect.

August of 1980, my parents helped me move my stuff into my dorm room and college life began. Being away at school gave me a taste of freedom. I was free from my dad and his ranting, raving and abuse. After my first year away at school, however, I realized the costs of school had become more than I could afford. It was apparent I would have to move back home if I was going to finish my college education. I hated the thought of going back "there," but figured since I would be so busy with work and school; I would hardly ever be home. I convinced myself that moving back would work out, or at least I hoped it would.

I moved my belongings back into my childhood home (I use that term loosely), and took over the bedroom in the basement. Things went okay for about a year. I worked part time as a sales associate at Macy's in the Cumberland Mall and attended Georgia State three nights a week. I was not home much and thought everything was fine.

It was a clear, crisp fall day in October of 1981, when out of the blue, my dad came into my room. He told me that my mom had decided that I needed to move out on my own. He didn't tell me her exact reasons but I was fairly sure it was not solely her decision. I didn't know why I needed to leave, but I was pissed off and relieved at the same time. For the next couple of weeks, I looked for a cheap apartment along Roswell Road. I began working full time at Macy's and started taking a lighter class load during the week night. Life was crazy busy, but I was getting by and doing what I needed to do to make ends meet and get through school.

Life at this point was filled with work, school and friends. I would say that things were fairly mundane until one cold, winter day in 1983, when I received a desperate phone call from my brother. His voice was shaking and he told me he was tired of the pain and informed me, in a whispered voice that he was going to take his life.

Kris had been thrown out of my parent's house when he graduated from high school because of his drug use and lifestyle choice. He was currently working as a maintenance man at a rundown Cobb County apartment complex. He lived in a small one bedroom apartment on the premises. Kris, by this juncture in his life, was pretty much a full blown alcoholic and drug addict. He appeared to be stoned and/or drunk each time I saw him.

His tiny one bedroom apartment was nasty and smelled of old cigarettes and stale beer. I did not visit him much, but when I did, there always seemed to be a random person passed out on his couch. I guess they were his friends but I really did not want to know any details.

After the frantic phone call from my brother, I jumped in my red Volkswagen rabbit and drove to his apartment. I ran inside and found Kris. He looked as if he had not slept, eaten or bathed in days and I could tell he was high. He told me he felt like he couldn't live with his skeletons and demons anymore. I knew Kris was overcome with emotional pain, but I didn't know what to do to help him, but I knew I had to do something. I decided we were going to go and find help. I decided to drive to the local Police Department. I had always been taught that if you had an emergency situation on your hands, a safe place to ask for help was the local police or fire department. So that is where I headed.

After about a ten minute drive, we arrived at the Smyrna Police Department. A few seconds later, I got Kris out of the car and into the lobby. I took a deep breath and was relieved I was able to get Kris here safely.

Behind the glass window in the lobby was a large police officer with a flattop and a protruding gut. Of course, in my mind, all I could think about were all those doughnut jokes told about cops and this dude totally fit the profile. This plump officer's name tag read Officer Cook. I told Officer Cook what was going on and why we were here. I then handed him my drivers license as he requested. I thought that was a rather strange request, but I did as he asked of me since I was there asking for help.

Officer Cook then proceeded to asked for some identification for my brother. I got Kris' license and handed it to him. He disappeared for a few minutes then opened the secured door that was leading to the lobby. As he came out of the door, he handed me back both driver's license. He looked at my brother and told him to stand up. I had no idea what was happening, but I knew it was not good. Officer Cook told me there was an outstanding warrant for my brother's arrest and he was being taken into custody.

As the officer placed Kris in handcuffs, I kept repeating that he was in severe mental distress and needed psychiatric help. I pleaded with him and repeatedly told him that Kris needed to be stabilized before taking him into custody. Officer Cook just ignored me and as Kris was walking away with him, I had a sense of overwhelming disappointment blanketing my entire body. Why can I not count on the people I should be able to trust? Who can you trust in this world?

The sullen look of disgust on the officers' face made me feel like I was a criminal. I asked to speak to his supervisor and was told to have a seat and that someone would be out shortly.

About twenty minutes later, Sergeant Ferrell walked out and asked how he could help me. I told him what had taken place and in a patronizing tone, he assured me that Kris would be just fine. He said that he would be placed on suicide watch and an officer would be checking on him frequently. He also said that he would personally make sure, that all items Kris could possibly use to harm himself would be removed from his cell. I felt a bit better, yet it still was devastating to leave Kris there. I knew he was already feeling so lonely and scared when I brought him to the station, and now this. I got home from the police station around 11:00 pm, took a hot shower. I sat down on my shower floor and cried. I cried for my brother and for myself. I cried for our lost childhood and for what my brother had become. I cried to cleanse myself of the hurt and guilt I felt for taking my brother to the station. I felt betrayed by those officers. This betrayal brought back a lot of garbage that I had pushed deep down inside.

I finally had dozed off to sleep when my phone rang about 2:00am. I jumped up out of the bed and looked around trying to figure out what was making that loud noise. I looked to my right and realized the phone by my nightstand was ringing off the hook.

I answered the phone and Sergeant Ferrell was on the other end. He sounded very upset as he told me that my brother had been transported to Brawner's Hospital about an hour ago. Kris had somehow taken apart the toilet in his cell and repeatedly cut his wrist with a piece of metal. Anger flooded over me, and I began screaming at Sergeant Ferrell as loud as I could. This was exactly what I had feared. I interrogated him about the officer that was supposed to be keeping close watch on him? Why all the precautions I had been promised earlier were not followed? What the hell happened in that cell. Who was in charge of making sure my brother did not hurt himself? Sergeant Ferrell was unable to answer any of my questions.

At sunrise, I called my mom to let her know the details of last night. I told her that my brother had attempted suicide and had been taken to Brawner's Hospital. She basically asked me the same questions I asked Sergeant Ferrell. Just as he was unable to answer my questions, I was unable to answer hers.

That next day, my mom and I met in the mental health hospital's parking lot. We were going to see Kris. She and I walked together arm in arm into a sterile white building that used to be a big Victorian home. It was converted into a mental health hospital about 20 years earlier. It was a beautiful old building, but on the inside, you could feel the pain and suffering of those who had been admitted and who temporarily called this place home.

As mom and I signed in at the front desk, we were greeted by a kind, but overwhelmed looking female nurse with graying hair and a half crooked smile who told us to have a seat. We sat down on a much worn light blue velveteen sofa that needed new cushions and springs. This couch had obviously been sat on by many anxious people waiting to see their loved ones. Some would learn of good news and some would leave knowing that their family member or friend may never make it home. We were not sure what news we were going to hear in relation to my brother, but were hoping the news would be positive.

About twenty minutes after mom and I took a seat on a dilapidated sofa in the waiting area, a doctor came out and introduced himself as Dr. Dial. He was an older gentleman who looked to be in his sixties. He had salt and pepper hair, a gray beard and a soft and calming voice. He told us that my brother had tried to commit suicide last evening. He was found by one of the officers as he was lying on the floor bleeding profusely. An ambulance was called and he was transported to the nearest emergency room and stabilized before arriving at their facility. Dr. Dial did his best to prepare us for the serious condition my brother was in. He informed us that because Kris had lost so much blood, we would find him extremely pale and weak. He may also be somewhat incoherent as he had been heavily medicated in order to keep him relaxed and help him sleep.

Despite being warned, as we moved through the locked door leading to his unit, my knees grew weak, and nearly gave way as I entered the room and saw Kris lying there. Doing the best I could to hold it together, I walked to his side and gave him a hug. I could see that his skin was a yellowish color and he had black circles under his eyes. The circles were so dark he looked as if he had been beaten in the face. I couldn't hold back the tears. When Mom bent down to hug him, she lost it too and tears began streaming down both our faces. Kris laid there motionless. His face was blank and showed no emotion. I understood that he had been medicated, but the sight of him lying there in that bed looking so hopeless was almost unbearable. It took me back to that night when my brother was beaten so badly by my dad. I had so many emotions spinning inside of me. I could not process this suicide attempt. I felt myself "shutting down" and the walls I had built around myself, getting taller. This seemed to be the only way I could survive another tragedy.

As I looked at Kris lying helpless in that hospital bed, I wanted to hunt down my dad and show him the damage he had done. I wanted to walk into his church and inform all those folks that looked up to him as an upstanding Christian man that my father was a son of a bitch. He was a man who had beaten his family so frequently and so severely that the bruises left behind had scarred our bodies and our souls. I wanted to show them pictures of my brother who was sedated and in a mental hospital thanks to their beloved Brother Jay. All of this however, would be impossible as I had no idea or desire to seek out the man I had called dad. Several years before my brother's suicide attempt, my mom and dad finally divorced. I cut all contact with him and never wanted to see him again unless it was for an apology. He had to ask for my forgiveness and prove to me he had changed. I would not hold my breath.

About a week later, Kris was released from Brawner's and I placed him in Ridgeview Institute, which was known as one of the best recovery centers in the Atlanta area. I was hoping Ridgeview would give Kris the help and support he needed to change his life. I was aware such a change was completely up to him and I did not have a lot of confidence in his desire to do so.

Over the years, Kris had convinced so many doctors and professionals his drug and alcohol problem was not that bad and he would work the 12-step program from home. He promised he would attend Alcoholics Anonymous meetings every day and meet with his therapist once a week. He did a great job manipulating the system again and was released about two weeks after he entered the Ridgeview Program. I knew it was a matter of time before he started down that same old addiction path again.

About a month after Kris was released from the hospital, I received a certified letter in the mail from the Police Chief in Smyrna. It was an apology letter for the events that led up to my brothers' suicide attempt. The letter informed me that Officer Cook and Sergeant Ferrell had been reprimanded and suspended for one week without pay. A letter documenting the reprimand was also added to each of their personnel files. I looked at that letter several times. I grew angrier each time I read it. I finally folded it up and threw it in the fireplace so the next time I lit a fire that event would go up in flames. I wanted all the horrible memories of that day to go up in smoke. How dare he write me an apology letter? It was too late for that. The Chief was probably afraid I would sue his department and sent this letter to look as if he was truly concerned about my brother and our family. It was too little, too late.

CHAPTER SIX

It may appear to some that the unpacked memories of my life have been a series of events that are tragic, heartfelt and just plain ol' sad. There are many happy moments tucked away inside my suitcase as well. I will dig one out now.

As I search around in my case I run my fingers over some type of book. It has a smooth, yet pebbled feel to it. I pull this item from the case, and as I look down, I see a beautiful white book with gold lettering on the cover. It is my wedding album.

The year was 1986 when I met the man that I would marry. His name was Carr Pacilli. Carr and I dated for about a year and a half before we walked down the aisle. I was so head over heals in love with this guy. I thought I had met my knight in shining armor. I was clueless to the fact that deceit and disappointment was looming around the corner.

Our wedding was fabulous and the first 10 years of our marriage were filled with fun, adventure, success, friends and travel. I will focus most of this chapter on the good times and then move into the not so good times. I will also examine my inability to see things clearly until the marriage was over.

Looking back, I realize those first ten years were not as wonderful as I first recollected. Also, after some serious soul searching and self awareness, I began to see that I had put on the same type of performance that I had as a child and protected this man until I could cover for him no more. This is the story of Carr and Patty.

For the next three years after my brothers' attempted suicide, I worked at a real estate development company in the Buckhead area and moved into a really cute townhouse in

Dunwoody. I continued to go to school at night and was content with the business of a busy life. I was out on my own, supporting myself, and enjoying success and independence.

One afternoon in August, life would change as I knew it. I was sitting in my apartment after being at the pool all day when the phone rang. On the other end was Becky Gillam. Becky was a longtime family friend whom I had known since I was twelve years old. She and my mom had, at one time, worked together at a flexible packaging company in the accounting department. She and mom became fast friends and worked together for about two years. Becky was now working at another company (Becky seemed to be laid off a lot) with a woman who had a son named Carr.

Carr was single and with Becky knowing both families so well, thought that Carr and I would make a great couple. Becky decided to call me on that Saturday to see if I was currently dating anyone. If not, she wanted to introduce me to a guy name Carr. She thought Carr and I had a lot in common and would get along very well

I sat quietly on the phone and thought for a few minutes. I told her that it was okay to give him my phone number and she did. About two hours later my phone rang again. Carr was on the other end. We talked for about thirty minutes and seemed to have a lot in common. Before we hung up, he invited me to join him and his friends at Taco Mac for dinner the next evening. I told him it sounded like fun and we agreed he would pick me up at my apartment around 7:00pm. I didn't give too much thought or have too many expectations of Carr other than he seemed very nice on the phone.

The next morning, it dawned on me that I needed to go shopping to find something cute to wear on my date. I had not dated anyone on a steady basis in quite a while, and realized that I only had work and play clothes in my closet.

As seven o'clock approached, I was dressed in a yellow, off the shoulder, cotton sundress feeling pretty and ready to go. I began to get really nervous waiting for Carr's arrival so I decided to drink a Heineken beer to help settle my nerves. At five minutes past seven there was a knock on the door. When I opened the door, I was greeted by the sight of a handsome, dark headed, green eyed man. His muscular arms were bulging from beneath a pink polo shirt he was wearing. Hmm, this could be a very good date.

As Carr stepped into my living room, he complimented me on my appearance then told me I may want to change. He said his friends dress very casually and he did not want me to feel overdressed. I told him that it was just a sundress and I was not worried about what everybody else was wearing.

We talked and laughed all the way to the restaurant. When we arrived, several of his friends were already at an outdoor table enjoying a pitcher of beer. Carr introduced me to everyone and we joined their table. I was offered a glass of beer and gladly accepted. After two beers, I noticed Carr hadn't been drinking. I asked him if he was going to have a beer. He told me he was allergic to alcohol and he was just going to have water. When our waitress came by, I detected a tone of arrogance in his voice as he informed her that he did not drink. It would not be until a decade later that I realized this should have been my very first clue. I should have known then that something was wrong with the way Carr reacted.

After dinner, Carr took me home and we basically shook hands at my front door and he left. As I went to bed that night I was flushed and giddy. I really liked Carr and he seemed to be a very nice guy. I wanted go out with him again and hoped he would ask.

Carr called me at work on Monday afternoon. He knew that I had school on weeknights, so he asked if I would like to get together on Friday. I was thrilled to be asked out on a second date with him, and I even felt the flutter of butterflies in my stomach.

As I arrived home from work Monday afternoon to change clothes and head downtown to Georgia State, I saw someone sitting on the stairs in front of my apartment. As I got closer, I could see that it was Carr. He was holding a beautiful bunch of fresh cut flowers. He stood up from the stairs, reached his hand out, and told me that the bouquet was for me. I took the flowers and thanked him, but told him that I could not visit then because I had to get ready for school. He said he completely understood and would see me Friday night.

Everyday as I arrived home from work, Carr would be sitting on my apartment steps, holding fresh cut flowers for me. I was speechless. He was so kind and thoughtful and he just swept me off of my feet. Everyone who knew me saw that I was smitten and my mom even said "I think this may be the one."

Carr and I dated for about 5 months and in December of 1986; our conversations began focusing more and more on life as a married couple. It was "when we are married" we are going do this and "when we are married," we are going to do that….. Carr never technically got down on one knee and proposed, but we did go to a jewelry store at Cumberland Mall and picked out a small diamond ring and a plain gold wedding band. I was just beside myself with excitement and my family was thrilled.

About six months before the wedding, in June of 1987, I was having hard time putting money together to pay for our wedding. My mom had agreed to help some, but since Carr was 29 years old and I was 26 and both worked full-time, we felt that we should foot most of the bill for the wedding.

Since Carr and I really were just starting out and did not have tons of money, I decided to do some professional babysitting on the weekends. I looked under sitting services in the phone book and found a sitting service that I thought would be perfect. I contacted the service, filled out all of their paperwork, and was put on their list of preferred sitters. That weekend, after I had been approved. I received a phone call. The service told me that they had an assignment for a 11-year-old girl who lived off of West Wesley Road in Atlanta. I told them that I would take it.

At 7:00pm on a beautiful Saturday night in June, I found myself ringing the door bell of an incredibly huge brick mansion in one of the most exclusive areas of Atlanta. A tall man answered the door and introduced himself as James Barnesfield. He led me through the maze of his home, which looked like it came straight out of Veranda Magazine. The tour ended at an indoor pool. As I walked into the pool area, a young girl popped her head up out of the water and introduced herself as Maddie. After I introduced myself we continued our tour. I felt like a cornbread girl in a caviar world. I was so overwhelmed and somewhat intimidated. Several times I checked my feet to make sure they were still on the ground. The reality of my life was just a few miles away in Dunwoody. Nevertheless, I made up my mind to enjoy this experience while it lasted and not take one thing for granted.

The experience lasted for quite a while. Maddie and I hit if off so well that I quickly became the Barnesfields exclusive sitter. I was at their home at least three times a week while they went to the opera, ballet, and entertained artists from around the world in their home. This was a whole new world opening up for me and I was taking it all in. I wanted to emulate this family as much as I could. They represented what I believed was a "normal" family and not a "screwed up one" like my own. The Barnesfields treated me as a part of the family and allowed me to enjoy many things with them.

Although, it was just an average day in their life, it was always an amazing, new experience for me. They were so good to me that I think of them and feel such much gratitude. They supported me throughout college, and worked my sitting schedule around school.

Many times when I would arrive home after a day of sitting, I would reach into my coat or sweater pocket, and there would be a random twenty dollar bill slipped in the pocket. I had an inkling that Mr. Barnesfield had put it there. Yet to this day, twenty five years later, he still refuses to acknowledge that he knew anything about this "magically appearing money." Let me tell you, this money was much needed and greatly appreciated.

It was now October of 1987, and I was about to lose my mind. I was going to school at night, working during the day, babysitting all weekend and trying to plan and pay for a wedding. It was a couple of months before the big day, December 12th, and I still could not find a place to hold the reception, or at least a place that Carr and I could afford. With our budget, we may have been able to afford the event room at Ryan's or rent out the local Moose Lodge (joke). Neither were options, however, and as my stress level continued to climb and I did my best to hide my concerns from Mrs. Barnesfield. When she asked me if the wedding details were completed, I told her that the ceremony was taken care of, as well as, the dresses and flowers, but we still were looking for a place to have our reception. She told me that she had the perfect solution for my problem and offered her beautiful home for the reception. As tears formed I tried my best to hold it together but found her offer almost too hard to believe. She told me that I was part of their family and that she truly appreciated all that I had done for Maddie. It was the least they could do for Carr and I. This was the first time anyone had ever done anything this kind and thoughtful for me. Here was this loving, generous family opening up their amazing home for one of the most special occasions of my life. I did not feel worthy to accept such an incredible gift, but she insisted, and I said that I felt honored.

A month before our wedding day Carr and I went out with Karen and Kevin Campbell, who were my best friends from college, to celebrate our upcoming marriage. They wanted to go to the Beer Mug in Brookhaven, which was basically a dive bar that served cheap beer and played beach music. Karen, Kevin and I were really into shagging and loved this place. We would go and dance for hours on end. The one great thing about Carr not drinking is that we always had a designated driver to get us home safe and sound. Carr like feeling important and we obliged him.

After leaving the Beer Mug that night we headed to where we had parked our car and noticed there was a boot on our tire. We looked around and did not see any "No Parking" signs where we had parked. Carr saw the boot and became furious. He called the number on the side of the boot and told the person on the other end that they better send someone to remove the boot from his car immediately or they would be sorry.

About ten minutes later a young man drove up in a red tow truck with Rick's Towing printed on the side. We waited for the fellow to park and step out of his truck but it seemed as though he was taking his time just to antagonize us. Carr walked quickly towards the tow truck driver and began to yell profanities at him. When the driver told us that it was going to be one hundred dollars to unlock the boot on the tire, I thought Carr was going to rip the guy's head off. Scared and thoroughly embarrassed, I just wanted to pay him and go home. Karen and Kevin told the driver that they would walk to a nearby bank machine to get some cash. The tow truck driver got in his truck and waited for them to get back.

By that time Carr had calmed down, he was waiting on the other side of the tow truck. I was glad he was keeping his mouth shut and no longer verbally abusing the tow truck dude. When Karen and Kevin returned from the ATM, they were heading toward the side of the truck were Carr had been standing. Karen's eyes got huge and there was a look of fright and shock on her face. I had no idea what was going on as Karen paid the driver.

The tow truck driver proceeded to unlock the tire and he got the hell out of there. Carr and Kevin decided to go into the IHOP and use their bathroom. Karen and I sat in the car and waited for them. Karen was really quiet since she and Kevin returned from the bank and I asked her what she was so upset about. She asked me if I had seen what Carr did to that tow truck. I assured her that I had no idea what Carr was doing. I was just happy that he was quiet. She told me that when they came around the corner from the bank she saw Carr stabbing a knife into the tow truck driver's tire. With a look of fear in her eyes Karen warned me to watch my back. She told me that I might want to reconsider my decision to marry this man. Of course, I did not listen. Eventually, the guys returned and Carr drove everyone home. The ride back was awkwardly silent. The tire incident was not mentioned again until years later. We all pretended it never happened.

By this time in my life, having been trained as a child to masterfully keep secrets, I was an awesome actress and quite convincing. Committed to upholding our image of perfection, I would never mention to Carr that I knew what he had done to the tow truck or to anyone else for that matter. I made excuses in my mind that he was tired that night or just getting nervous about the wedding. I fooled myself and it worked. The wedding was going forward as planned and my life was perfect, or so I had convinced myself and all those attending.

The day was December 12th, 1987.....my wedding day. The evening before the nuptials, I had spent the night at my parent's house in Douglasville. This was necessary because it would be just plain obscene for a true southern lady to see her groom the day of their wedding.

That morning, as I got out of bed and entered the kitchen, I smelled bacon and biscuits cooking. A flood of memories flooded over me. I was not going to let anyone or anything, including memories of the past, ruin this special day for me. Nevertheless, it was a challenge to be in the house that had so many sad memories.

I watched as my mom scrambled eggs in a giant cast iron skillet and checked the biscuits to make sure they did not burn. I was finding solace in her morning routine. I sat down at the table to enjoy the comforting event with her. She looked over at me, smiled and said "Are you ready for your big day?" "About as ready as a bride can be, I think."

She joined me at the table and we ate breakfast together. We talked about last minute details and things we needed to get done before the ceremony. I asked her where dad was and she said told me he had gone to the Barber shop to get his hair cut.

I sat in my old bedroom later that morning, getting my gifts together and writing a few thank you notes. I did not want to be overwhelmed when I returned from my honeymoon. I heard my dad walk into the house and he made his way back to the bedroom where I was sitting. I looked up at him and almost pooped in my pants at what I saw! He had gone to the barber shop and gotten an ultra curly poodle perm. He looked like a total frigging idiot! I could also tell that he was jacked up and appeared to be in a maniac state. He looked around the room at all the gifts, and out of the blue asked if he had to come to the wedding reception. I was not completely surprised until he said, "Oh and by the way, your mom said she wanted all this crap out of here right now."

He walked out of the room and I sat motionless and began to cry. I knew he would try and take away any happiness I would experience today. I quickly dried my eyes and decided he was not going to ruin this day for me. I would hold my head high and ignore his game playing. I gathered all of my things from my childhood home and headed to the church. I was relieved knowing it would be the last day in this house as a Blackwood. I was leaving this name and identity at the back door for good.

Mom arrived shortly after me at the Second Ponce DeLeon Baptist Church Chapel around 4:30pm. The wedding would start at 7:00pm sharp. Our wedding director met us at the front door of the church and introduced herself as Mrs. Martha Preston. She was a typical Buckhead housewife and had played this role with pride for over forty years. Her husband, Peter Preston, was a prominent cardiac surgeon at Piedmont Hospital and they lived on Habersham Road in a lovely brick Tudor. Her lawn, as well as, her nails was manicured to perfection. Mrs. Preston volunteered as the wedding coordinator for the church so that she could give back to her community. She fit the role like a true southern belle and had an accent that sounded like she had pebbles in her mouth. Mom and I looked at each and both grinned at her southern charm. Oh how I love the south!

The florist was in the sanctuary placing all the poinsettias in the beautiful stained glass window sills. As I peeked in their floral boxes, I could see white snowballs with the red velvet ribbons that each bridesmaid would carry. Most girl's in the south chose May or June to have their wedding, but I decided on a Christmas wedding. This was the one-time of the year that I consistently had happy childhood memories. I also picked Christmas because I knew the chapel would be decorated for the season. Since Carr and I didn't have much money to spend, I took advantage of the flowers and candles, already placed in the Chapel. Each of my attendants would wear a forest green velveteen Laura Ashley dress (tea length so that it could be worn again) and each groomsman would wear a black tuxedo, a plaid cummerbund and a red bow tie. The flowers, dresses and all other church decor complimented each other just perfectly.

I went into the bridal dressing room at the church, and put on my $50 J.C. Penney Outlet Store wedding gown and $10 veil with a five foot lace train, and the picture taking began.

My attendants and I had a champagne toast and before I knew it, it was show time. I hiked up my dress with all those crinolines underneath and headed towards the door. I had no idea what to expect as my dad walked me down the aisle, but was petrified to see his new poodle top.

Surprisingly, the ceremony went perfectly without incident and my dad did not cause any type of a ruckus. Carr and I were officially married, but before we could begin our new life together, more pictures were taken of the wedding party. Then we walked half a block from the chapel to the Barnesfields home for the reception.

I walked up the front stairs of that familiar home like I had done so many times before, but today, it felt totally different. I was now a married woman. I could feel my whole body tingling. Was this a dream? Could it be that this girl who had been through so much heartbreak and was so used to be treated as "less than," was walking into this beautiful mansion surrounded by friends and family? I almost had to reach down and pinch myself to make sure this was real.

I quickly composed myself and noticed that the front door to the home was open. Carr and I walked inside and were greeted by Mr. and Mrs. Barnesfield. As I entered the formal living room, adorned with a priceless art collection, I noticed that music was being played by a retired high school teacher of mine sitting at the beautiful, shiny, black grand piano. I looked around the first floor of the home and could not believe my eyes. There were magnificent floral arrangements placed in every nook and cranny of each room. White roses, orchids, and lilies graced all of the tables, fireplaces and doorways.

I approached Mrs. Barnesfield to say thank you but she just smiled and told me that they do this every year for Christmas. I knew that she had done this for me. I was speechless. I was not used to anyone doing something for me solely from the kindness of their hearts. There was no way possible that I could ever have afforded something this grand. My heart was full.

I looked around and saw the people I loved most in this world. For the first time, if only for a few brief hours, I did not feel any pain, fear, or guilt. My past was not invited to the wedding or reception, and I did everything within my power to keep it locked away. I focused on a future full of love and peace with my new husband.

The day was deemed a success by all. The only issues we had in regards to the wedding was with Grandma Rosetta. She had flown in from San Francisco. She did not want to come into a Baptist Church since she was a staunch Catholic. We luckily, got past it after she met me and she determined I was alright in her book. There was also the photographer my dad hired who ran out of film about an hour into the reception. Who has ever heard of a wedding photographer running out of film? I am not sure how much we paid him but obviously it was not enough for him to purchase adequate supplies. I was simply relieved that my dad kept his crap together for the day.

As Carr and I made our way to the front door to leave for our wedding night in a honeymoon suite at the Ritz Carlton Hotel right down the road, Mrs. Barnesfield pulled me aside. She and Mr. Barnesfield had a wedding gift for us. I was very surprised. She had already provided her beautiful home for our reception and had flowers arranged and placed all over the house just for this occasion. She told me that I had been such a help to them when they needed it most and that I was a part of their family. I was very touched but felt that anything else they did would be way too much.

As I teared up at the kind words from Mrs. Barnesfield, she handed me a crisp cream colored envelope with a card inside. I opened it and found a hotel reservation made for us at one of the most exclusive hotels in London for a real honeymoon! The reservation read "one-bedroom suite with fireplace and dining room table" and "a dinner reservation at the hotel's 5 star restaurant, Le Gavroche."

Carr and I had planned a trip to England (he had lots of frequent flyer miles). We would stay a couple of days in London and then travel to the Cotswold's so we booked a room at The Lambs Inn on Sheep Street in Burford. We had saved about $500.00 for the entire honeymoon. The available credit line on our MasterCard would not begin to cover the cost of dinner, and certainly would not cover the cost of the suite. I could not thank her enough for this amazing gift and was so personally touched by their kindness and generosity.

On Monday morning, after the wedding, Carr and I flew into Gatwick Airport in London. We were picked up by a car sent by our hotel. After a short ride, we arrived at the Mayfair District of London, and were greeted by several members of the hotel staff. The concierge opened the car door and welcomed us to 47 Park Lane. We got out of the car, shook everyone's hand, and were escorted to our suite. As I walked into the foyer, I could not believe my eyes. This suite was the size of our townhouse. There was a real wood fire burning, and the huge mahogany table in main living area was covered with breakfast and snacks. It was just more than I could ever image.

We stayed at this phenomenal place for two days. We ate at the five star restaurant our second night there. After our meal was finished, I prayed to God that when we checked out the hotel, the bill was in no way going to be charged to us. The next morning as Carr and I stood at the front desk waiting to check out, I was perspiring like crazy. I felt my knees go limp from relief and almost cried when the front desk personnel informed us that the account had been paid in full by Mr. and Mrs. Barnesfield and thanked us for our stay. Whew! These words were music to my ears.

Carr and I sat in the hotel lobby waiting for a cab to take us to a near by bus station so we could head to Burford. As I glanced over to my right, I saw a man that looked so familiar and he was smiling at me. The man walked up to us and all I could say was "it's Moses." Yes, it was Charlton Heston and all I could do was continuing saying "it's Moses" as if I were in some kind of trance.

Mr. Heston was very hospitable and asked us if we were on vacation. We told him we were on our honeymoon. He offered tickets to see him in *A Man for All Seasons* playing that evening at the Palladium. We chatted for a moment, and then told him we could not accept his kind offer as we were headed to the country to spend the remainder of our honeymoon. He wished us well and we all went our separate ways. I was certainly hoping that this was a sign of good luck and a reflection of better things to come.

CHAPTER SEVEN

I must move on and reach into the case again to see what memories and secrets are next. I sift through my pajamas, bathing suit, and old t-shirts until I find an old bank statement on white paper with a blue logo. I remember now, this statement is from the Trust Company Bank. I pull this piece of paper out and review it carefully. It's a bank statement from the second year that Carr and I were married. Wow, how did we survive on so little money? I don't know exactly how we did it, but what I do know is we got by just fine.

The first few years that Carr and I were married, we both worked very hard at advancing our careers. Although we were barely scraping by, we were as happy as two peas in a pod. He worked as an industrial engineer at a uniform rental plant. I worked several different administrative jobs.

About three years after we married, Carr met a co-worker of mine whose boyfriend was a salesman at a large software company and was wildly successful. Carr was intrigued by this man and said "I am going to get a job doing what he does and I am going to make lots and lots of money." He put out resume after resume and worked so very hard to make this dream come true.

About six months later, Carr was hired at a small software firm. He was ecstatic because all the hard work he had put into graduating from Georgia Tech was now going to pay off. The software company he was going to work for only hired out of MIT and Georgia Tech. Carr felt that he was on his way.

After a year or so, while working his heart out, Carr slowly became successful. However, it seemed like the more success he achieved, the more he became a stranger to me. I did not like this emerging person. At the same time, I did not like the person I was becoming either. I was starting to forget where I came from and where my roots originated.

The bank statement from my case reminds me, sadly, of two people who started out so in love and the enticement of success and money put both of them on different paths. These separate paths would eventually bring them both to the end of the road. Not even love could survive entitlement and arrogance.

It was a very hot and humid summer day in August of 1989. Carr and I woke up early among piles of clothes, household items, and tons of boxes. Today was the day that we would purchase and move into our very first home. We bought a traditional; two story brick home in the Smyrna area. We purchased the home directly from Mr. Moon, the builder. It was a brand spanking new home that had sat vacant for about a year, so Mr. Moon was very motivated to sell. He offered a lease purchase so that we could get our money together over the next few years. He would give us a credit at the end of the lease period to use for our down payment. We were so excited and saw this as the perfect opportunity to buy our first home.

We closed on the house and moved all of our stuff from our townhouse into our new home. Things were looking so promising for the two of us and I could hardly wait to have our first family get together to proudly show off our new home. It was such a great day! We worked on our house just about every weekend. We were painting inside and out and making it our own. We wanted to get rid of the boring eggshell color the builder had put on the walls.

Unfortunately, for some unknown reason, I felt as though I was a connoisseur of paint colors. When I look back at the pictures of the rooms I painted, I realize that I had the ability of a blind moose to pick out colors. My kitchen was painted a bright sunflower yellow. I was going for a "butter yellow" look but sorely missed. The kitchen looked more like a school bus than any stick of butter I had ever seen.

The living room was painted a "puke" pink which answered my question as to why I would get nauseous every time I walked into the room. Wow, I am so glad that I have acquired some taste since then (I hope), but I was young and thought I was as talented as Martha Stewart (this was of course before her unfortunate incarceration). After looking at these old pictures, I was not.

Nevertheless, I loved my home and was proud to entertain. I enjoyed having friends and family over on a regular basis. We even had Carr's sister Casey's wedding and reception at our home. It was a good time in our marriage.

Carr and I were just living life to the fullest and enjoying our home, our family and friends, and his software job. About five years after starting his software career, he was honored with the sales consultant of the year award at the corporate sales meeting held in Vegas. He received a plaque, a bonus and qualified for the Club trip to Hawaii in the spring. I was so proud of him and could hardly wait to take my first trip to Hawaii (hi-why-ya to southerners') with all expenses paid. Life was good.

Carr had worked very hard to earn this honor and the only major drawback was he was never home. Our lifestyle was definitely changing. We were able to travel more, but that was about the only time we had together, and even then, he would bring his laptop with him and work for most of the vacation. We had more and more money to spend on the house, cars, travel, and entertaining, but less time to be together. I could basically purchase most things I wanted, within reason, and was having a blast driving my new Mazda Rx-7 convertible and shopping at Tiffany and Co.

With Carr and I becoming more financially stable, I began getting bored with my administrative position. We no longer needed my income so Carr and I both decided I was due for a change. I tendered my resignation at the real estate development company; I had worked for the last 5 years, and returned to college at Georgia State to finish my degree.

I stopped attending college after Carr and I got married. I figured we were doing just fine without finishing my degree. As Carr was climbing the ladder to success at his job, we both felt that it would be a great time for me to finish college. I felt a void in my life and Carr had made it clear that he did not want children. I knew I needed to do something for myself that would be satisfying and give me a sense of accomplishment.

In 1993, I decided I would go back to Georgia State and pick up where I left off. I would go full-time and I declared my major in Social Work. For the next few years, I worked hard to get through school. I was required to do a Social Work internship before I could graduate. This in itself was well worth returning to school. I got a lifetime of experience in just nine months interning in the Social Service Department at Grady Memorial Hospital in downtown Atlanta.

I began the first day of my internship at the hospital, and I was extremely nervous. With Grady being the county hospital for those who were uninsured and those who could not afford medical attention, I really did not know what I had gotten myself into. I observed that most of the patients and employees were African American and did not know what to make of me. I was a pasty southern girl with a thick southern drawl and red hair to boot.

I parked my sky blue convertible in the hospital parking lot and walked over to the children's hospital which was a division of the main hospital. As I walked across the street, I looked over to the main entrance of Grady. There were patients standing everywhere. Folks were wearing their hospital gowns and rolling their I.V.'s by their side as they smoked. Some were getting food at McDonald's, and even walking to a nearby liquor store and coming out with a little brown bag. As I took all of this in, all I could say was "what the hell?" I began to wonder if this internship was going to be the longest nine months of my life.

Passing the strange and somewhat chaotic scene outside, I walked into the Social Services office and was greeted by

Phyllis Washington, the Social Services Director. Phyllis was a very attractive black woman with her hair pulled back in a perfect bun. She wore a navy blue business suit and looked as though she could have been a model in her younger days. Her features were very sharp and her smile was so big that she lit up the room.

She showed me to a small office with two desks. It looked like it had previously been a closet. This was where I would do my paperwork and charting.

About five minutes later, a black woman with braids and a rye smile walked into the tiny space that was referred to as my office. Ms. Washington informed me that this young woman, Ms. Thompson, would be my mentor. She encouraged me listen to everything Ms. Thompson had to teach me since she was one of the best social workers in the hospital.

My mentor appeared to be a very kind, yet spunky, teacher. On the first day she informed me that I would be functioning as an integral part of the Social Services team until my internship was done. I was so excited about what awaited me; I eagerly grabbed my files as we headed to the emergency room.

The two of us walked into the busy, packed, and bustling emergency room and were immediately called over by a young medical intern. He told us that he had a case that needed to be investigated asap. The intern was treating a three year old boy who had a large burn on his face in the distinct shape of an iron. Ms. Thompson and I walked over to this little boy's bed and pulled back the light blue hospital curtain. Sure enough, there was well defined iron imprint branded on his tiny, sweet face. It appeared as though someone pressed a very hot iron to this child's cheek. At the very moment I saw that innocent baby's face, I felt like I was going to throw up. Who the hell would do that to an innocent child? I quickly flashed back to the days of my dad abusing my brother, my mom, and myself. Even after all of the torture he put us through; I still could not fathom what kind of "sick" monster could hurt a child like this.

That's the kicker though... I did know. I grew up with this psychotic evil in my own home. My heart hurt so badly for this little boy. I knew the confusion and distrust he must have been feeling. It was hard, especially as a small child, to understand why someone who was supposed to love and care for you ends up hurting and discounting you.

I reached down and gave this little fellow a hug. A hug like the one that I needed after a brutal beating or a demeaning word. I had my momma to comfort me; however, she was usually not very responsive because she was trying to survive herself. She did her best and I now, as an adult, understand that. As a child, I asked God many times in my prayers, why my momma did not protect me. I did not learn the answer to this question until many years later.

Working with these kids was harder than I ever could have imagined. It brought up stuff that I buried for years. I had purposely pushed the toxic junk deep down inside so that I could get through my day to day life. As hard as I tried to keep it buried, some of it, resurfaced here and there. When it did surface, there was usually a depression that followed. It was a dark place full of hurt and sadness.

Nine months flew by so quickly and I successfully finished my internship. This experience showed me another side of life and I was so relieved that I made it through and held it together as well as I did. At the end of my internship journey, what seemed to be an awful mistake, actually turned out to be an amazing experience. It taught a little southern girl a lot about herself, and even more about others. People I would not normally have met in the circles in which I traveled.

After graduating college in May of 1996, I was trying to decide what my next step would be. Carr was still traveling a lot during the week for work, and since I was no longer attending classes, I needed to find something to do with my time.

There weren't many decent opportunities in the social services field at that time. By some crazy aligning of the stars, I was coerced by a friend to get my real estate license. She was actually the same friend who sold Carr and I our first home. She said that the market was hot and that many of my customers would share all of their problems while in my car looking at property. Because of my social work background, she felt that it would be the perfect job for me.

My friend sent me to real estate school to get my license with the agreement that once I successfully finished the course, I would come and work for her company. What the heck. It sounded like a good idea, so I got my license and went to work at Home Town Realtors. I must tell you it involved about as much therapy as my time at Grady. I was beginning to come to the clear realization there are a lot of miserable people out there. I was amazed at what people told me! I heard it all, good, bad, and lots of ugly.

CHAPTER EIGHT

It has been somewhat comical thinking about my experiences decorating my first home, interning at Grady, and the crazy folks I worked with when I was selling real estate. Before I can start digging through my baggage again, I need to go make myself some lunch (with my cooking skills it will be a peanut butter and banana sandwich) and take a short walk to clear some of the spider webs out of my head.

The cool, light winds outside are just what I needed to give me a shot of energy to work some more on my task at hand. I sit back down on my bedroom floor, lean forward into the case, and randomly begin to poke around until I find a copy of the Marietta Daily Journal Newspaper. This was our local community paper. It was a typical hometown paper, with political stories making the front page, obituaries, metro news, and just about anything else that would take up a few spaces towards the end.

As I look at the front page of this particular edition, I see a picture of myself leaning against a old oak tree in the front yard of the McLaren House. I loved this home so much. I also loved all the events, gatherings, and ghost stories that went along with owning such a historic home.

I continued to sell real estate for several more years and Carr continued to sell computer software. As our household income grew so did our desire to purchase a new home. We had been looking at different neighborhoods in East Cobb County and in the Historic District of the Marietta Square. There was one house in particular that we visited several times, and we continued coming back to this home. This particular home was located on N. Forest Drive in Marietta, and was quite a step up from our first home with a price tag of over $225,000.00. Never in my dreams, did I think we would be able to afford a home like this. We somehow pulled the money together, made an offer, and the next thing I know, it was ours

The house was over 80 years old, had 4 bedrooms, lots of intricate old mill work, and original mahogany hardwood floors. My favorite feature was the huge wrap around front porch, with a white washed swing, that looked out over all of the wonderful old homes and gardens that surrounded us.

On spring and summer evenings, many of the neighbors would come by and sit on our front porch. Depending on which of the neighbors showed up, would determine if we had tea or cocktails. One must remember that we were in the Bible belt and I was raised to show respect to others who may not partake in alcoholic beverages due to their religious views. On my porch, we tried to respect all different religions, but really liked when the Catholics, Presbyterians, and Contemporary Baptist showed up. Although Carr and I really liked our new home and our close knit neighbors, we both had our eyes on the prize. The prize was a civil war mansion that was located on one of the most prestigious streets in the Historic District of Marietta. I passed this home each day while I was out walking our two Airedales, Walter and Molly, and always wondered "what kind of folks live in a big house like that?"

Well, apparently Carr and I would be the kind of folks that would live there. About a year after first noticing this home, it went up for sale. Around that same time, Carr had recently been offered a new software sales position that included a huge salary increase and bonus plan. Our dream came true. The wonderful times we shared in our home on N. Forest Avenue were going to get even grander at The McLaren House. After our contract had been accepted and we knew it was going to be ours, I could not sleep that night. I was so excited, and felt so incredibly lucky to know that I was going to be the next owner of such a splendid home. Carr and I were moving on up and so were our egos.

It was October of 1998 when we closed on The McLaren House. The house had four large bedrooms upstairs with a huge landing and a mural of the original gardens adorned the walls in the common area. There was a sun room that overlooked beautiful boxwood and hydrangea garden, and a marble reflecting pond full of koi. The downstairs was comprised of a side entrance foyer, a men's parlor, a formal parlor, a large kitchen with a keeping room, and another sun room in the back of the house that ran the entire width of the home. I think this sun room was used as a ballroom many years ago, and then as a ballet studio for a previous owners' daughter. The front of the home had a large portico (porch for those of you who are not familiar with southern lingo) and four sets of ceiling to floor French doors that opened onto it,

I easily imagined about 80 years ago, Mr. and Mrs. McLaren hosting lavish affairs at this splendid home where all the French doors were open as lots of folks laughed, chatted, mingled, and perhaps even danced. I didn't know if any of this really happened, but it was fun to use my imagination to drift back into time. I felt so lucky to be a part of that magic, and somehow be connected to an era of such elegance, grandeur and romance.

As the new owners, Carr and I discussed adding a few of our own touches here and there, but all in all, the home was in very good condition. We eventually added a swimming pool in the side yard and enclosed the huge piece of land with a fence so that we had some privacy. Despite the perfection of our home, the location wasn't quite as perfect.

Carr and I were living in the city (where my original roots were planted), and we lived on a busy state road that had about 35,000 cars pass in front of our house each and every day. Although we lived in a historic district with other amazing homes in the area, behind our home about three blocks was the "hood." The hood consisted of many low income residents along with a housing project that was once considered an open drug market.

When we first moved in, we had a number of exciting (and not so exciting) events happening either in our back yard, our driveway, or up and down McLaren Street which ran parallel to our home. Occasionally, I would look out of our back sun room window and see undercover cops dressed in all black surveying the projects.

On another occasion, I walked outside to get the Sunday morning paper and found a woman slumped over her steering wheel in our driveway. Thinking the woman was dead, I freaked! I quickly realized she wasn't dead... she was just high. A few times, we had drunks passed out in our front yard. We usually let them stay and sleep it off as long as they did not cause any commotion. If we were having a party or other function, we would call the police to help move them along.

The McLaren home was perfect for hosting events and we often held or agreed to allow others to host birthday parties, political dinners, holiday celebrations, a citizenship party, and we even hosted Katie's wedding reception. I really loved to entertain and was pleased to open my home and celebrate so many special occasions. I have such wonderful recollections of these times together with neighbors, family, friends and even a few strangers who tagged along with some of the guests. Many good times were had and Carr and I worked well as a team. We loved entertaining and sharing in the special moments in so many people's lives.

Carr and I lived in the McLaren House for five years and for the first two years, things went fairly well. We were active in our local community, politics, symphony and neighborhood issues. I also did some volunteer work with the Marietta Police Department.

One of my favorite projects was "Take Back the Night" which was a community outreach program where participants walked down drug infested streets as a statement that we were going to take control of our community. We had food, music, speakers and prayers before we headed out. I coordinated this event for two years and found it very satisfying. I also enjoyed meeting many folks that had a misconception about the "rich" white lady who lived in the big house on the corner.

I served on several committees headed up by the Mayor of Marietta, and developed a clean-up program for "Lyman Homes" which was the housing project behind our home. Occupants of the property, neighbors, kids, and volunteers gathered on a rainy Saturday morning in the spring of 1990, and cleaned the grounds, planted shrubbery and flowers. We also started a "Yard of the Month" contest. Each month Winner received a $50 gift certificate to Wal-Mart. It was so inspiring to see young children plant flowers, many for the first time, and taking pride in their community. It was a good project.

The work that I was doing within the housing project caught the interest of the local newspaper, The Marietta Daily Journal. A reporter called the house one afternoon and asked if they could interview me in regards to my community work and talk about the history of the McLaren House. I agreed, and the reporter scheduled to be at my house the next day for an interview. A photographer would take some shots of the house as well. Although reluctant about the photographer, I said it would be okay even though it made me a little bit leery. I was very aware of how critical many of the Old Marietta residents (OM's) could be (especially those with new money). The last thing I wanted was take a chance on one of them making snide remarks around town or in print.

The reason I say this is that one day I was looking through the gossip column, Miss Marietta, in the paper, and low and behold I spotted my name. There had been an OM come, I guess during the night, and measure the siding on the detached garage we added to the house. She did not like that the new siding on the garage was a quarter inch different than the siding on the house. I could not believe what I was reading. That was why I was so reluctant to have pictures taken. Someone may not like my coffee table or the type of toilet paper I used (one or two ply). I thought about it for a while but then agreed to let the photographer come. Oh how I hoped I would not regret this decision.

As I became more involved in community activities and programs, Carr was working more and more and gone most of the time. When we were at home together, we were like roommates. He would either sit in his office and work on the computer or be on conference calls with clients. I would plead with him to come and swim with me for a bit, or go to lunch with me. Usually the response I got when asking Carr a question while he was working was a snapping of the fingers or a shushing as a way of letting me know that he was busy. I was certainly not a priority. As Carr worked longer and longer hours, we began growing further and further apart. His tone with me was often curt and condescending.

When trying to explain something to me, Carr would say, "Oh, I forgot that a lay person would not understand this." I could not believe his arrogance and his demeaning attitude towards me, his family, friends, and co-workers!

Eventually, I enjoyed Carr being gone all of the time and pretty much adjusted to my lifestyle. One day when I was sitting in his office downstairs working on the computer, I came across a postcard on his desk. I read the card and it was from a female that he had worked with in Alaska. I was initially planning to go on this trip with him as a mini-vacation, but about a month before we were going to leave, he told me all he would be doing was attending meetings. He said he thought I would get bored and would not enjoy going with him.

I read the writing on the back of the card, it said "Carr, I really enjoyed being with you in Alaska and I hope our paths cross again soon!!" I read this postcard over and over again and got that "uh oh" feeling in my gut. I felt something was just not right with our marriage. I continued to handle these suspicions in my usual way, and pretended that everything was fine. I had to once again make sure the secrets were safe. I mean, what would people think if they knew that my marriage was not perfect? It could possibly disrupt my whole existence. It is way easier to be in denial than to have to face the reality that my marriage was perhaps heading down a road that would eventually turn my suspicions into certainty.

As time passed by, I continued to sit in that big beautiful home alone, with my Porsche in the driveway and my bank account full. All the while, I attempted to ignore the enormous void in my heart. What was missing? Why can't I seem to fill my heart with all these things that I have.

I really should be ashamed of myself for bellyaching. It could be much worse. But, I still continued to cry at night, and put on a happy face during the day. I began to loathe this liar that was looking back at me in the mirror. I had all the material trappings a woman could want, but I was one of the loneliest people on this earth.

Nevertheless, I was determined to make my marriage work. I could not fathom the idea of divorce and refused to give in to my notions and assumptions, at least for now. I decided to work harder in order to make my facade look convincing. My crumbling marriage would be my secret and would not be exposed to others.

CHAPTER NINE

Wow! The good memories are getting me pumped and eager to move on to the next item. Returning to the suitcase, I retrieved a folded, yellowed, and worn copy of my birth certificate. I don't think I have ever really looked closely at this document.

Memories of my early years are very vague. I was not allowed to ask too many questions about my birth and the first years of my life. The only stories are few and far between. Most of the information is small tidbits I have gathered from eavesdropping on my mom during her conversations with family and close friends. As I glance down at this piece of paper I see my name, Patty Elizabeth Blackwood. At the very top of this official document printed in large letters is "State of Alabama." I am very confused because my birth name is different than the name printed on the paper.

I think it was during my early teenage years I began asking mom questions about my "real" dad. I wanted to know who he was, what he was like, and most important, what did he look like? It quickly became apparent to me that my mom did not want to talk about him, but she finally spoke of him briefly. She walked out of the kitchen and returned from her bedroom in the back of the house. She had an old, tattered, black and white picture of a handsome man in an army uniform. She looked straight into my eyes and told me "this is the only picture I have of your dad. Please take care of it and keep it out of sight." She told me not to talk about him in front of my adopted dad. We needed to keep any stories she told me to ourselves.

I fully understood what she meant by not wanting to rock the boat. In our home, you did not want to do anything to set my dad off. It was always a delicate balancing act. I knew it would be best not to talk about the past or anyone who had played a role in our previous lives. I put the picture in my dresser drawer for safe keeping. This was the only treasure I had of my "real" dad. Every now and then, I pull it out and think about him. I wondered if he was still alive, and if so, where did he live? What I wondered most was why did he leave us. Those questions would remain unanswered for decades, so I had to move on.

According to my mom, she had a tough upbringing and would have done anything to get out of her parents home. Sadie and Wayne Walters lived in a rural area not too far from the University of Georgia in Monroe. My papa owned an auto garage/salvage yard and my grandma kept the house, tended to the garden, and raised her three children. Money was very tight and, rumor had it, my grandpa drank a lot. When he got drunk, he was mean. When I visited them as a child, I never saw him take a drink; however, I don't know what happened behind closed doors. I have gathered, from comments I have overheard, that it was not filled with a tremendous amount of love, support or nurturing.

My grandma did the best should could to love and care for her children, but she had so much to do, and was spread very thin. I do remember my grandma standing over a hot stove in her little house cooking for us when we came to visit as children. She had arthritis so severely that her ankles would swell almost to the size of a cantaloupe. I knew she was in a lot of pain but she would have never let anyone know. She was a sweet lady and I adored her.

With such a harsh childhood, my mom was ready to get out of her home and go out on her own as soon as she could. She would hopefully find a place where she could give and receive the love she was so yearning for in her life.

While out one night cruising the local Freeze Queen with a high school friend, my mom was introduced to a very handsome and charming service man. His name was James. He was kind, charming, good looking, and showed mom a lot of attention. They dated for a short period of time and before everyone knew it, they were married and expecting a child. My mom was so excited to finally be out on her own and away from her parent's home and felt as though this could be the start of something new. At least that was what she was hoping for.

After having a small wedding at the Walton County Courthouse, my parents moved to Gadsden, Alabama where James's family lived. He was very close to his parents, grandparents, and his brothers and sisters. Shortly after the move, James found out he was going to be stationed in Germany for a year then would be heading to Vietnam, Mom was "very" pregnant and not able to travel so she planned to stay in Alabama until my dad was able to come home. Unfortunately, things did fall in place as planned. Shortly after my dad relocated to Germany, my mom received a letter from him. He had met someone else there and would not be returning home to her, her son, or to his newborn baby girl. My mom did not have time to feel sorry for herself so she packed up everything she owned and moved us back to Georgia.

These are all of the memories I have during that time in my life. These memories are just bits and pieces of stories that have been told to me or from overhearing conversations of family members. As I said earlier, I knew the rules and my boundaries, and I kept them.

I don't know if I have tried to forget the beginning of the end of life as I knew it or if I just do not remember in order to maintain some type of sanity. Hopefully, by unpacking this suitcase, some answers will come to the surface. The details and memories that have been tightly and firmly packed at the bottom of this bag. I know they will come out wrinkled and messy, but can eventually be worn with love and never put back into that dark, lonely place again.

CHAPTER TEN

I'm almost halfway through this tedious process of unpacking. I'm exhausted from the physical and emotional work that is involved in reopening these memories. I want to finish what I started because unpacking will allow me space for new things and ultimately, lighten my load for my next journey.

I look down at the remaining items lying in the case and know the hardest and most painful ones of my life are still waiting to be unpacked. All of these memories have been screaming to be released and put away. The weight has been too much for just one suitcase to hold. Stuff has been packed on top of stuff and shoved down down deep year after year. That is why I must continue to rifle through the contents of my life still waiting to be removed.

I'm not just talking about physical luggage. However, if I do not finish this journey I will carry this "baggage" for the rest of my life. I had to unpack and truly, honestly start the healing process. I need to complete the process and be done with it for good.

I noticed at the top portion of the case, there is an elasticized, zippered pocket. On the inside of the pocket, I found a road map. As I looked to see where the map would lead me, I saw Gadsden, Alabama, my birthplace.

On Tuesday evening in May of 1999, I was home watching TV in my bedroom and wondering what Carr was doing. I began dozing when the phone rang. A male voice on the other end asked for Patty Blackwood. I told them that I was speaking, but my name now was Patty Pacilli. There was a long pause before the caller spoke again and said "no" with a rather terse tone in my voice. The person was quiet again and I began to say "hello, hello, and hello." A few seconds later a voice came back on the phone and said "Patty, this is your dad." The voice did not sound like my dad and I told him so. "No this is your real dad."

I sat totally still and my brain began spinning and I felt sick to my stomach for a few seconds. I did not know how to handle this or what to say. I have been waiting for this phone call all of my life. I had so many questions and there was so much I wanted and needed to know.

We talked about trivial things for a few minutes before I asked him how he found me. He told me that he had a friend that worked for the Georgia State Patrol and he located me in their system after years of searching. He did a search and found a traffic ticket issued to Carr. It just so happens that my personal information was listed in the insurance section. Once he had my address and Social Security Number he was able to look up my phone number.

He asked me if it was okay that he called, and I told him I needed a few days to process everything. He gave me his phone number and said that he was living in Alabama. He also told me that if I wanted to talk to him further, I could call him collect. He would leave the ball in my court. When we hung up, I did not know if I would call him again or just ignore him like he had ignored me for the last 40 years.

I sat up that evening thinking about that phone call. Instead of sleeping, I tossed and turned and wondered about this man. The man who left me when I was born. What was he like? Did I look like him? What had he been doing for the last forty years? Did he ever miss me? Was he ever curious what I was like and what type of person I was? The questions in my mind went on and on.

As I thought of all of the things I had wanted to say to him, I felt excited, sad, confused, mad, frustrated and most of all curious. Why was he calling now? Did he ever try to find me during my childhood? I had so many questions and it dawned on me that the only way I would ever know the answers was to talk to him. I wanted to meet him and start getting answers. I decided that the following evening, if I could muster up the courage, I would pick up the phone and dial his number.

I called Carr and told him about the phone call. His opinion was that I not waste my time on a man who walked out on me and never bothered to have a relationship with me. He told me that he was meeting some of his business partners for dinner at a local pub. I told him alright and I hung up the phone. I thought it was strange that he would be meeting for dinner in a pub. He would pitch a fit if I ever suggested that we go and meet friends or family at a restaurant/bar. He thought bars were smoky and he could not breathe. He would say that he did not want to eat around a lot of drunks and blah, blah, blah. If he caused such a stink about going to a bar with me, why would he not be refusing to go now? This was just another example of things not adding up, but I had bigger and more important things on my mind and could not deal with his crap right now.

The next evening, I sat with the phone in front of me trying to find the nerve to pick up the receiver and dial. I tried several times, but hung up before I finished dialing the number. I took a deep breath dialed the whole number and kept the phone close to my ear. A woman answered. I asked for my dad and waited as I heard her say "It's your daughter, Patty." I never thought I would hear those words spoken. It was totally overwhelming, yet comforting in a sense.

James, my "real" dad answered the phone and told me that he was glad I called. I immediately started to cry and told him that I had so many questions to ask. He was overwhelmed too and not quite sure where to start. He kept saying that he was sorry, over and over again. He asked if there was any way I could drive to Alabama to see him. He wanted to answer all of my questions in person. I immediately told him that I would come the next day if he was going to be home. He said he was retired and was home on most days. The only exception was when he was receiving radiation for a throat tumor that he recently had removed. He would wait to tell me everything until then. He gave me his address and we hung up.

I went to a nearby Citgo and bought a road map. I needed to plot my trip to Alabama the next morning. This was another night I wouldn't sleep. As you can probably imagine, I was stressed and anxious for the morning to arrive and had no support to speak of. My mom did not want to hear about it, and all my husband would say is "why do you want to waste your time on that loser." I was on my own again, and quite frankly, I was glad.

I woke up bright and early on Thursday morning. I started getting ready for one of the biggest days, besides my wedding day, that I would probably experience. I decide on a pair of khaki shorts, a black Ralph Lauren polo shirt and a pair of Born sandals. I looked in the mirror and thought; I looked like I had stepped out of an ad from Talbot's. I grabbed my map, my cup of coffee, and all the courage I could muster, and jumped into my emerald green BMW convertible. It took me about 3 hours to get to Gadsden from Marietta. I drove down Padenrich Avenue, then turned onto Maryhill and began to look for the house number that he had given me the night before. On the right hand side of the road, I saw the house number that I had been looking for. I stopped in front of a light pink, asphalt shingled home with a small front porch with chairs for sitting. I parked my car on the street and headed for the front door. My legs shook. I was doing everything possible to hold it together.

I knocked on the door and waited for what seemed like an eternity but was only a minute or two. A dark headed man with brown eyes and very light skin greeted me at the door. I could hardly believe what my eyes were seeing. I felt I was looking in a mirror, however, I was looking at my dad and there was no doubt, where I came from. I really did not know what to say or how to start a conversation, so I just jumped in with both feet and started asking questions. We talked for hours and hours. I learned that he had married the woman he met in Germany, and they moved to California where he lived for many years. I found out that I had several stepbrothers and stepsisters out west, but they don't have anything to do with him. He told me that I had lots of aunts, uncles and cousins in the Gadsden area. He could not believe that I looked so much like his side of the family.

We talked about my Scottish ancestors, his health, his girlfriend Ruby, and we just went on, and on. I did not want to leave, but knew I had a long drive home and needed to hit the road. Ruby invited me to stay the night, but I did not feel comfortable yet. Home was where I needed to be. I gave him my address and some other information and headed towards the door. He walked behind me and reached his hand out to me. As I extended my hand towards his, he grabbed me. He hugged me so hard that I thought I would lose my breath. We both cried tears of sadness, regret and joy.

The front door to his house closed and I sat in my car and attempted to pull myself together. I began to drive towards the interstate with streams of tears still pouring from my eyes. I drove slowly home because I had four decades of tears that needed to come out. I slept for about twelve hours that night and woke up the next morning with a very peaceful feeling. I knew who my daddy was and realized that the milkman was not my father after all.

Several weeks went by after my road trip, and I had talked to my dad a couple of times. We really just talked about superficial things and did not get into anything too deep. I must admit that it was kind of fun hearing stories about my grandparents, aunts, stepbrothers and sisters and other family members. I did realize that my dad did not give me a lot of details about his past.

He did not appear to have a lot of substance as a person and really did not seem to have any close relationships, except for maybe Ruby. They had lived together for the last five years as both of them had been married several times. They each did not have any desire to get married again. They kept each other company and that was good enough for them.

About two months after our reunion, I invited my dad and Ruby to come up and visit me and Carr. We would have lunch and spend the afternoon visiting and learning more about each other. Our plans were confirmed and dad told me how excited he was to finally get to meet my husband. Carr and I worked very hard the week before his visit to make sure that the house looked great and planned out a lunch menu to die for. I had everything in place for the visit and then the phone rang around 9:00am. It was my dad and he told me that he was not feeling well and he and Ruby were not able to make the trip. I told him that I understood and we hung up. I have to say that deep inside I felt very let down and disappointed. He did not seem to make an effort to really get to know me, my husband, and the in's and out's of my daily life. I realized I was not very that impressed with him, but the real kicker happened about a week after that canceled visit.

It was a Friday morning, Carr was out of town as usual, and my phone rang bright and early. I usually would not pick it up this early and let it go to voice mail, but with the timing of this call, I thought someone could be hurt, sick or some other type of news. On the other end was my dad. He told me that he needed to ask me a big favor. He began telling me that he was having a very hard time financially and that he was about to lose his home. He stated that he and Ruby would be out on the street if they lost their house. He was aware that Carr and I were fairly well off and was wondering if I would loan him a large sum of money.

I was stunned and taken back. I had only met this man two months ago and here he was asking me for money. Was that why he wanted to meet me? Did he know that Carr and I had a little bit of money? Was he looking at me as his personal banker? His request made me madder than a wet hen. I told him that I did not have a lot of liquid cash and that most of our assets were tied up in real estate. The bottom line was that I did not have large sums of accessible money. I would have to liquidate stuff and was not prepared to do that at this time. He became somewhat curt with me and proceeded to hang up the phone. This whole scenario frustrated and disappointed me.

Here, I thought that I was possibly going to have a relationship with my birth father, but instead, he was more interested in what I could do for him financially. I knew then why he was a sick and lonely man. If the truth be told, he was a user and a manipulator. That was the last phone call I ever received from my dad. After talking to him and meeting him in person, I wondered what my mom ever saw in him: Did she truly fall in love or did she want to get away from her childhood home. Did she choose the first man who came along? These are questions that I know will never be answered.

Dear reader, you would think that I would be used to disappointment by now, but I really was holding out hope for a relationship with my dad. One that included brothers, sisters, aunts, uncles and cousins. I so wanted to be a part of a family that had the same flesh and blood as me. I had dreamed this dream for years.

Unfortunately, I just got more of what I had gotten in the past. Nothing but hurt, heartache and emotional abandonment. It was at that moment, I realized that I had been living by the old adage "if you do the same thing over and over, you will always get what you always got!" I was getting tired of the same result, but did not know how to change my life patterns. The void in my life was ever present and getting bigger. I continued to feel hopeless and confused, but I began to hear a voice saying, "I am still waiting." I, ignored that voice and the void in my heart remained open and raw.

CHAPTER ELEVEN

As I look back on all of my unpacked items. I find myself laughing, crying, and justifying things. I have purposely ignored lots of stuff in an attempt to make the task more "bearable." In doing this, I keep returning to a common theme: complete and utter disappointment. Disappointment with my family, friends, church, and so many others that I cannot begin to list them all. I've been told I have a tendency to set unrealistic expectations for people. My response is always while their belief may be true, I have no idea what a realistic expectation is because my lowest ones are rarely met.

Turning my attention to the suitcase after having recognized my repetitive theme of disappointment in my life, I'm not surprised by the next item: a scribbled note... This note forever changed me and was pivotal in my ability to face my demons and to learn the meaning of true forgiveness. The contents of this note would bring me to my knees and help me to rise again.

It was a rainy and cold March morning in Marietta. I was standing in my kitchen and could feel the chill from the wind coming through all of the cracks, leaks, and uneven door jams of the big old drafty antebellum home. No matter what we did to try and seal off as many spots as we could, our gas bill ran about $900 a month during the winter. Both Carr and I were outraged when we were told by the gas company that the house was billed on a commercial rate due to the square footage. I argued with the "weenies" at this Marietta Power for several years until they finally wore me down to a nub. So we sucked it up and paid the bill during the coldest months of the year. This was the price we paid to live in a historic home with over 7,000 square feet. To this day it makes no sense to me, but it was not worth my time or stress fighting with the bureaucrats.

Carr and I were in the kitchen discussing our plans for the day when our phone rang. I figured it was our friends calling to tell us they were going to be late picking us up. All four of us were going to the International Auto Show. I picked up the receiver and said, "Hello." I said it several times but no one responded. After about fifteen seconds, I continued to say hello over and over again, but received no response. After about 15 seconds, I hung up the phone and was quite irritated that someone would be so obnoxious as to call and not say a word. I stated my frustration to Carr and thought nothing more of it.

As we waited on our friends to arrive the phone rang again. I became annoyed, stomped over to the phone, and answered with a harsh tone. On the other end a man asked to speak to me. He was very matter of fact and had absolutely no inflection in his voice. It was a Sheriff's Deputy from Douglas County calling with some bad news.

By this time a million things were running through my mind. Had my brother been found and arrested again? Was there a car accident? My mind was still racing when the officer informed me that Jay had just committed suicide. I felt my knees start to buckle beneath me and slowly I sat down on the floor. The tears started flowing as I asked him for whatever details were available. He told me that Jay was at home and went under the deck in his back yard. He put a gun in his mouth and pulled the trigger. The one shot blew his head off. He was pronounced dead at the scene. He told me that his wife Jessie was the one who found him.

I don't remember hanging the phone up. I do remember my legs giving in to my weight as I collapsed on the floor. I was not sure how I was supposed to feel at that moment. Do I feel hurt, mad, or relieved? Who do I call? What do I say to my family? I wasn't sure where to start, but I did know that my heart was hurting. Despite all the painful memories, he was still the dad that had raised me. I cried so hard that I was barely able to breathe. I let out a piercing yell that almost shook the rafters of my home. I didn't understand why this news hurt so much.

Carr was back in our sun room watching the news while waiting on our friends to arrive. He raced to the kitchen when he heard me sobbing uncontrollably. He thought I had fallen and hurt myself. I looked up at him with tears flooding down my cheeks and told him that "my dad had just shot himself, blew his head off, and was dead." As I sat on that cold kitchen floor and looking up at Carr, I was stunned a second time by his cold response. "Well good riddance. I'm glad he's dead. I think I will go to the cemetery after the funeral and pee on his grave." These cruel words felt like a second blow, I got myself up off of the floor and attempted to compose myself.

I called my mom to see if she had been given the news. The phone rang several times before she picked up and answered. I could tell by the raspy sound of her voice that she had been crying. She told me that she had just gotten off the phone with the Douglas County Sheriff's Office and they informed her of the suicide. I asked her what we needed to do. She told me that she was going to call my sister, Katie, to see if she had been called and then we would go from there.

I knew Katie was going to be devastated by the news. Katie had been Jay's golden child. She was the only natural child that Jay had and he definitely showed more love, attention, and patience towards her. She was spared from the beatings and had a totally different reality growing up than my brother and myself. This news was going to rock her world.

After I hung up the phone with my mom, my cell phone began ringing. I looked down to see who was calling. I really did not want to be bothered by anybody right now. I did not want to have to explain why I was crying and feeling waves of sadness. Could the world just leave me alone for a minute? It was the call I had been dreading since being informed of Jay's death: It was Katie. My mind started racing again. What do I say to her? Can I get through this without totally losing my grasp on reality? Can my family pull it together and just love each other without allowing the past to rear its ugly head.

I stopped the questions in my mind and answered the phone. I decided that no matter what happened over the next few days, I was going to put my anger, rage, and hurt aside. I must be a strong, steady support for Katie, and most of all, allow myself to grieve the loss of the only dad I have ever known.

When I hit the talk button on my phone, I heard Katie crying. She cried harder when I said hello and began gasping for air. I tried to calm her down and told her to catch her breath. I quickly realized that she was in the midst of a severe panic attack. I continued to tell her to breathe deeply until finally she calmed down. As her breathing returned to normal, she asked me if I knew that dad was dead. I told her that I had received a call from the Douglas County Sheriff's Office. She asked me to come to Jessie's house so that we could be together. She begged and pleaded for me to come right way. Her request was a difficult one to accept. I had not spoken to Jay in over six years and had separated myself physically and emotionally from him. My purpose for doing this was to maintain some type of normalcy in my life. His sister, Sara, blamed my mom, Kris and I for deserting him and felt we were the root of all of his recent troubles. Sara never saw my dad as anything but perfect. Many years later, I discovered from my cousin Rosa, that Aunt Sara displayed a lot of the same "sadistic" characteristics as Jay. Although I questioned if I was strong enough to face the giants of my past, I knew that that I would do anything for my sister.

I put on my coat, got in my car and headed to Douglasville to be with Katie. On the way, I started working on my acting skills. I wanted to make sure that I put on a good show for family, friends, and past church members that I had not seen in over twenty years. As I drove up in the driveway of

Jessie's two story brick traditional home off McGowan Road, all I could say to myself was "let the show begin."

I stepped out of my Silver Jaguar and walked up the long driveway. It felt as though this "walk of dread" would never end. I had never been to Jay and Jessie's home. The house was a large two-story brick traditional with a three car garage. It sat on a small hill and it appeared that the lawn had been taken care of by a landscaping company. There was a newer dark blue Volvo sitting in front of the garage door on the left, and a Dodge Ram truck sitting in the middle bay. I was overwhelmed by the things I saw. One can only imagine the thoughts rushing through my mind as I walked towards the front door.

I couldn't help but wonder why Jay had bought such a fancy house, had nice cars in the garage, and a yard service. The man I knew did not believe in living "high on the hog" as he would put it. He did not believe in driving new vehicles, or heaven forbid, having a company manicure his lawn. The first steps into this house were some of the hardest steps I have ever taken. I am sure that learning to walk was probably not as hard as this moment in my life. I kept saying to myself "just put one foot in front of the other and hold steady."

As I steadied myself, I began to look around the room. I became aware that I was in the formal living room. The room was furnished with two full length sofas, a club chair, several end tables, lamps with fringed shades, and custom made window treatments. It appeared to have been decorated by a professional. I was about halfway through the living room when I saw a shadow moving quickly through the adjacent dining room. This shadow headed down the hallway in a hurry, and then disappeared out of sight. I was not positive who it was, but I had a sneaky suspicion that it was Aunt Sara.

After my mom and Jay divorced, my Aunt Sara basically wrote mom, Kris and myself off. We were no longer acknowledged as a part of her family. She felt that my mom had deserted my dad and he had been suffering from a broken heart for years. I wondered if she now blamed us for his suicide.

Continuing to walk slowly, I headed to the doorway leading into the kitchen and could hear hushed voices and words of encouragement. Before I could step into the room, I saw Katie coming towards me. I grabbed her and we hugged for what seemed to be an eternity. I could taste the salt from the tears rolling down my face. As we let go of each other, I could see that almost everyone surrounding us was emotionally touched and reaching out for us.

One woman put her hand on my shoulder. As I turned around and looked at her, I realized that it was Mrs. Hamby. I was in Sunday school with her daughter for many years and I had a huge crush on her son Todd when I was in high school. Todd and I went out on one date and all I can remember was that he loved Paul McCartney and we listened to the Wings cassette over and over that evening. I don't think that we went out again but I was totally infatuated with him for at least a few months and then it was time to move along to my next teenage crush.

Mrs. Hamby hugged me and kept telling me how good it was to see me and how sorry she was for the loss of my dad...such a fine Christian man. As she said those words to me, it was all I could do to hold myself together and not shout out, "No! He was a child abuser, an evil person!" Instead, I reminded myself that I was there for my sister and I could grieve in my own way when I got home. I could scream, cry and grieve for myself and the fact that he would never be able to tell me that he was sorry. Sorry for the beatings, verbal battering and berating.

I would have to work through the steps of grief, but for now, I needed to be helping Katie get through this tragedy. I would worry about myself later. That always seemed to be the way I operated....others first...me last. For some reason, I always took the adult role in the family and helped everyone else work through their issues and problems. I don't know if it was because I was the middle child, or if it was just part of my determination to protect my spirit. I really don't have a clue, but I know that it sometimes gets very tiring. Having to make decisions for my family was often times a burden, but through my guilt, I did what I could to listen, help, and encourage. It was very hard and not fair. Why did I have to hold everyone's hand?

I continued saying my hello's, and hugging my family. I cried more than I had the last time I was beaten by the man being immortalized that day. I cried tears for my mother, my brother, my sister and myself. It was a very bittersweet time. The family I had always dreamed of was gone forever and there would be no fairytale ending. I sat in that house and listened to warm and fuzzy stories the mourners shared, and in my opinion, put on an academy award performance. I would make sure that no one would see the helpless, vulnerable little girl standing before them still looking for someone to love her unconditionally.

I heard the hallway bathroom door open and a voice say, "Sara, are you going to come in and say hello to your niece?" Sara was sitting in the family room and yelled into the kitchen "I have already said hello to Katie." Suddenly, Jessie walked into the den and said to her "Not Katie, but Patty." From what I could hear in her muffled voice she said, "I don't have a niece by that name, but if I did, I would die before I spoke to her. She is the reason we are here today. Jay died of a broken heart."

As I listened, I began to feel a tightening in my chest and knew I was about to lose it. My earlier question to myself was now answered. I realized it was all about to hit the fan and that I needed to get out of that house. I had nothing to say to this woman. I did not want to show any disrespect on that awful day and certainly did not want to get into this family junk. I did not have to defend myself to her or anyone else who wanted to share their opinion about my mom or me. I refused to get sucked in.

I hugged Katie goodbye and told her I would see her at the funeral home later that evening. I told her that I had things

I needed to take care of and if she needed anything, to let me know. We hugged again, and I walked out the door and vowed never return to that home again. I got in my car, broke down in tears, composed myself and then headed home. This day was only halfway over and I still had the funeral home that evening. I prayed for strength to get me through this ordeal and to keep my mouth shut.

I headed towards I-20 and turned my radio up in an attempt to and drown out everything that was swirling in my head. My brain jumped from one thought to another and overwhelming feelings followed each thought. I kept having flashbacks of being jerked out of a dead sleep and beaten as a child, my brother pleading and screaming for dad to stop pulverizing him. I could see my mom sitting in a fetal position on the floor rocking and begging my dad to stop hurting her children. These visions kept going round and round in my head. The more they circled, the louder I turned up the music in an attempt to make them stop. They did not.

Around mid afternoon, I pulled into the circular cobblestone driveway at my home in Marietta. I was relieved that Carr, who had gone to the car show without me, was not home yet. The last thing I needed was to hear his hateful commentary on my dad. Instead of getting hugs and support from him, I would be expected to justify why I was upset and crying. I felt like no one would understand that just because he was a real jerk who beat and tormented us, I still felt grief and needed to mourn the loss of the only father I had ever known.

I walked into the foyer and sat down on the stairs that led to the landing and bedrooms. I put my head in my hands and began to massage my temples. I could feel an awful headache coming on and hoped that that the rubbing would give me some relief. It was then that I realized that I had not eaten all day. There were plenty of casseroles, mac and cheese, jello molds, and pies that the church members had prepared and brought to Jay and Jessie's house.

Several women offered to make me a plate to take home and kept telling me that I needed to eat. The last thing they wanted me to do was lose my strength and end up sick. I appreciated their concern, but food was not on my mind until I arrived home. Carr came home while I was in the kitchen eating graham crackers and drinking milk. I cringed as I heard the foyer door open. My quiet solitude had come to an abrupt end.

He walked into the kitchen and began telling me about the awesome new cars that were on display at the Auto Show. He went on and on until he finally looked straight at me and said, "So how was your day?" I kept thinking to myself: how do you think my day was you ego manic. Let's see, my dad committed suicide, I had to go to his home and console my sister. My Aunt Sara then locked herself in a bathroom and blamed me for his death. I have to go to the funeral home tonight to hear more about this church deacon and beloved saint. How do you think my day was you giant prick! But instead, I looked at him and plainly said "it was difficult and sad."

All I knew right now was that I was beat and just wanted to take a long, hot, bubble bath in my old claw foot tub. Before I could clean up my crackers and milk, Carr began lecturing me. He couldn't understand why I was so sad over Jay's death or why I even bothered going to Jessie's house. "You should be having a party with champagne and caviar. That mean, terrible, son of a bitch is dead" he told me. "Do I have to go with you to the funeral home, or can I stay here and clean out my sock drawer?" I didn't bother responding to his nasty questions or comments. I had been married to him for so long that I knew when to keep my mouth shut. If I did not agree with what he said, I would have to listen to another tirade about not being on his side. He would tell me that I did not support him in his thoughts and actions. It was not worth a fight right now.

After taking my bath, I stood in front of the closest trying to decide what I was going to wear. I had not seen a lot of people who would be at the funeral home in years. I wanted to make sure that I looked darn good when I walk into that place. I wanted to disprove all the rumors that my dad had spread since I had broken off all contact with him. I chose an outfit that would send the message that I was doing well and in no way a crack addict or prostitute (that was what he told folks). My dad loved to spread untrue gossip. He tried in every way to convince people that it was not his fault that we did not have a relationship. I finally decided on my dark blue pin stripped Ralph Lauren suit as my armor. I was ready for battle.

I dried my hair, put on my makeup, got dressed, and preceded downstairs. I wanted to know if Carr was going with me or if he was going to stay home and "work," or do whatever he does in his office until wee hours of the morning. Although he was pissed off that I asked, Carr reluctantly agreed to go with me.

We pulled into the funeral home parking lot in our brand spanking new white Mercedes Benz sedan. We were dressed in our Sunday best and looked the part of an educated, sophisticated, upper income couple. On the outside we appeared to have it all. Carr opened the front door of the funeral home and we walked in to a huge crowd of mourners. I looked around at the sea of people and could not believe what I was seeing. Who were all of these folks and where did they come from? When I was a child, the only acquaintances that my dad had were men and women from our church. He never had old buddies that he told stories about, or work friends that came for dinner or visit. I was totally baffled as to why there were so many people there.

I felt someone grab my left arm and turned around to see that it was one of my best friends from high school. She was there with her mom and dad, and they all came over to me to tell me how sorry they were about Jay. I hugged all of them and thanked them for coming. We chatted for a few minutes and got caught up on all the Douglasville gossip. I began to realize it was time to leave my comfort zone and move closer to the room where Jay laid in his casket. As I walked through the crowd towards the viewing room, It was like stepping back in time. I could feel the waves of panic towering over me. There were sweat beads forming at my hairline, my chest tightened and my breathing became shallow less and frequent.

I took several short breaths and eventually began to feel my chest loosen. I was able to take a few more steps towards the man who almost destroyed me. The room where he was lying was surrounded by well wishing, kind, and loving, unknowing mourners. I could not be angry with these folks for being there, since I had been part of the "show." The show that convinced folks we were the perfect family who had just experienced a life shattering event and grieved for the one they loved. Deep in my heart, I wished that the man they came to grieve was really the person they thought he was. He was not.

I knew who he truly was and the horrific things that he had done to me. Would I ever be able to shut the memories and visions out of my mind for good and move towards serenity? I hoped that knowing this man could never hurt me again would lead me to solace and healing. The entrance to the viewing room was right in front of me. I slowly entered not knowing what to expect. I walked up to the casket and noticed that several people, who were viewing the body, stepped aside. I heard someone mumble under their breath that I one of Jay's daughters. I looked to my right and saw Jay's old, pale body lying in a rosewood coffin with an ivory, satin lining. I grabbed the side of the casket to help hold myself up. He was wearing a blue blazer, crisp white shirt and a red tie. I thought to myself that he looked so old and sad. Once again, thoughts started buzzing around in my head. Did he kill himself because he could not live with what he had done to his family? Did he tell his current wife, Jessie about his skeletons? Did he abuse anyone else after we were grown up and left home? Did he kill himself to get attention such as the crowd of mourners that gathered? The questions kept coming until I forced them to stop. Only Jay and the good Lord would know what truly happened on the morning of his death. At that moment, I surprised myself by praying that he had made peace with himself and my loving God had mercy on his soul. I stepped away from his lifeless body, and suddenly felt pity for him.

Heading back to the lobby of the funeral home, I stopped and spoke to several people I had known in my previous life. They all told me that I looked great, that I had not aged a bit, and that life was certainly agreeing with me. I thanked them and moved towards the sofa where Carr was sitting. As I reached the sofa, I plopped down beside him, leaned over and said, "We have get to get out of here. I cannot take any more comments about how my dad was such a fine, loving father and dedicated Christian servant." I told Carr that one man said, "You must be Jay's daughter since you look just like him." He said that my dad talked about me and my brother all the time. He told me Jay truly regretted that Kris turned out like he did. He had the nerve to say that he tried to help him for years to get clean and stay out of jail but could not save him. That was such bull malarkey. It was because of that man that Kris turned to drugs and alcohol to self medicate and try to forget the living hell he was put through as a child. I had to get out of that place before I puked or hurt somebody. All I wanted was to go home, get in my bed, and start all over again in the morning.

When we were finally home, I put on my long plaid flannel pajamas and turned on the television to help take my mind off of the events of the day. I surfed through the channels and found the Dr. Phil Show. Now, I'm not one who believes in coincidences, I believe that everything happens for a reason and was orchestrated from above.

That evening, the Dr. Phil Show was about true forgiveness of others and learning how to forgive unselfishly. I felt like Dr. Phil was speaking directly to me. Sitting still in my bed, I hung on every word he said. Dr. Phil talked about healing, forgiving, and finding peace. He spoke right to my heart and I knew I was never going to be able to heal until I gave true forgiveness for all the things my dad had done to me and my brother. If I continued to harbor this anger and hate, I would be the one who suffered. I would never move past the pain of my childhood and become a truly free person in both heart and mind. Without forgiveness, healing cannot begin and my heart would never open up to love. A huge lesson had just been dropped right in my lap. Thank you God.

I turned off the television, went to my desk, and got out a couple of sheets of notebook paper. I sat down and started to scribble some random notes. As thoughts and ideas came pouring out, it was apparent that I was in the beginning stages of writing a note to my dad. Once I finished my scribbling, I got out a clean piece of paper and wrote the following:

Dear Dad,

I am writing this letter to let you know that I forgive you for hurting me physically, sexually, and emotionally as I was growing up. It was time for me to start to leave the past behind and work on my future. You are no longer in control of my life. I will start moving forward today. I am sorry that you felt you had to take your own life and I will always love you. You are the only dad I have known and I thank you for that. Your daughter, Patty

As I dried the tears, I folded the note into a small square and stuck it in the pocket of the simple, black dress I would be wearing to the funeral. I did not know what I would do with the note, but felt the need to take it with me. I took a Melatonin, rolled over, and slept more peacefully than I had in years.

CHAPTER TWELVE

The sun was beginning to peek in through the shades in the master bedroom. I stretched, yawned, and rolled over to see if Carr had come to bed last night. Sometimes, he would stay up all night working, or so he said. Just as I suspected, the other side of the bed was empty and the covers had not been disturbed. I must admit I was kinda glad that he had not been there. I really didn't want to hear any of his hateful or mean comments. I was very well aware my dad was a psychopath, but today was the day I would do my best to remember the good times we had with him, which were few and far between.

I pulled the sheets back and put my feet on the cold hardwood floor. As I stood up, I could feel my muscles aching. I had held my body so tight at the funeral home last night, I was actually sore from the tension. Each time someone would come up to me and tell me how lucky I was to have Jay for a father, I could feel myself tense up. Based on the way I was feeling that morning, there must have been a slew of folks saying that. I could hardly stand up straight. There was certainly some Advil in my immediate future.

I shuffled into the bathroom, peed, took some pain relievers, went downstairs and put a pot of coffee on. It was going to be a "full pot" coffee morning. Hopefully between the Advil and the coffee, I would feel like a new person and be able to face the day with strength and determination. I poured a large cup of "joe" and proceeded to the back sun room to watch the news and see who had been shot who in the Atlanta area last night.

I rounded the corner and entered the back room that overlooked our boxwood garden and marble koi pond and saw Carr sound asleep on the big, comfy denim sofa. The sofa faced the outside windows and, quite frankly, was one of the best seats in the house. He was bundled up in his navy blue Georgia Tech blanket and looked like he was in a peaceful sleep. I sat down in the brown leather chair next to the sofa, and turned the television on to Channel 2 Action News. I had been watching Monica Kauffman for as long as I could remember. I had been through all of her hair styles and colors and it appeared that her latest style was a blonde, cropped cut. When I first glimpsed at her and the new haircut and color, I thought that Dennis Rodman was on the news. No kidding, Monica looked so much like Rodman that she could have been his twin.

As I looked over at Carr sleeping, I could see him stirring just a little and he was showing signs of beginning to come out of this deep sleep. Slowly his eyes opened and he looked over at me and said "good morning. How did you sleep?" I told him that I slept great. I wanted to stop any commentary on why I should not be sad or upset that my dad was dead. It must have worked since he did not respond. I sat in that sun room for about an hour, drank coffee, and tried to enjoy my last hour of normalcy. Soon I would head to the funeral and endure day two of the "martyr show" where my dad had the starring role. Heaven help me to once again keep my head held high and my mouth shut. Trust me this was easier said than done.

After getting ready, I went downstairs and asked Carr if he was going with me. It was hard to believe I had to ask my husband if he was going to the funeral of one of my parents. He said if I wanted him to go he would, but if not, he had no desire to go and bid farewell to the biggest "douche bag" he ever had the pleasure of knowing. I thought long and hard about my answer but told him that I needed him to be with me. I wanted my husband to be my ally among all of the mourners.

He reluctantly agreed to go and we headed out to make our appearance at the event that had overtaken the small town where I had grown up. People would be attending the funeral from all over so they could pay their final respects to one of the "most upstanding" men in their community. A sheriff's deputy had been hired to direct traffic because a huge number of people were expected to attend the funeral of deacon, beloved father, and upstanding church leader, Jay Blackwood.

Carr and I arrived at the funeral home at around 9:45am. We gave ourselves plenty of time, because with Atlanta traffic, you always had to leave early. One never knew if there would be road construction, accident or any number of things that could cause a major delay. The last thing I wanted to do was to walk into the funeral late and draw more attention to myself than already will be generated by my making an appearance. I felt an arm come behind me and begin to guide me towards the viewing room we were in the night before. Carr walked beside me and as I turned the corner, Katie came up to me, put her arms around my neck and began to cry so hard that I had to remind her to keep breathing. She looked up and into my eyes and said, "I really did not think you would come. Thank you, thank you." She grabbed my hand and led me to a circle of my family members. They were getting ready for the family prayer and the final goodbyes before the casket was closed and rolled into the service.

A large middle aged man with gray hair and a dark gray suit led the group in prayer. Once he finished, dad's wife Jessie, walked up to each family member in the circle and made a personal comment to each person, one by one. When it was my turn, Jessie walked right past me and never acknowledged that I was there. I could not believe she would stoop to that level. Who did she think she was? She had no idea of the hell and torment Jay put my entire family through. I should just give her a piece of my mind or better yet, I should get my stuff and leave.

Unfortunately, I was stuck there in that place. I had promised my sister I would be by her side no matter what, and a promise was a promise. I stood there stunned, and embarrassed, I felt an arm go around my shoulder. It was Katie's husband, Marco, reaching out to let me know that everything was going to be alright. He non verbally reassured me that I had done the right thing being there for my sister and most of all, being there for myself. This man was my dad too and I had every right to be there. I also had something I needed to do and I was bound, bent and determined to accomplish that feat. Today would be the beginning of my healing no matter what!

The prayer was done and the funeral director asked if anyone would like to spend a few minutes alone with Jay so they could say their final goodbyes in private. I threw my hand up as if I was bidding on a precious painting at an auction. Everyone turned around and looked at me with different expressions on their faces. Aunt Sara looked totally disgusted while Katie, Marco and several others teared up. They knew there were probably some things that I needed to say without an audience.

Everyone shuffled out of the room and waited in the foyer for their turn. I heard the door close behind me and a feeling of confusion totally overtook my body. Where would I start? How was one supposed to feel at the loss of an abusive parent? I loved this man because he was my dad and he worked very hard to provide for our family. We had the things we needed and wanted and honestly we had a very comfortable life as far as material things went. I also hated this man for the sick and violent way that he treated mom, Kris and me. I loathed him for beating us up physically and emotionally and for doing everything within his power to break us down and destroy any chance we may have had for a normal, healthy future. He took my childhood away and for that, I will always be haunted. Always searching to heal that little girl who was so scared and so innocent. It was time to do what I had come to this room to do.

I slowly walked up to the casket. I felt my arms and legs beginning to shake and my heart was about to come out of my chest. I reached down in my dress pocket and pulled out the folded, scribbled note that I had written the night of the Dr. Phil show. The note that would start my quest for peace and forgiveness. I took that small, tear stained piece of paper and slid it in the inside pocket of my dad's blue blazer. I looked at him lying there pale and frail and said "I forgive you dad. I will always have a place in my heart for you, but it was time for me to realize that you no longer have control over my life. It was time for me to start healing and begin to leave that little girl behind and start becoming the woman I am meant to be. Goodbye dad. I hope you are in heaven."

With that, I walked towards the door, opened it, and never looked back. It was time to start walking in the light and leave the darkness in the room where that sad and lonely man was lying. Katie and I walked arm and arm into the chapel and sat on the front row. The pastor from my childhood performed the service and when it was over, we all gathered in our cars and headed to the cemetery for the burial. I kept telling myself it was almost over and prayed that the angels would surround me and give me peace. Once my dad was put into the ground, I hugged Katie and Marco tightly and headed towards the car.

Before I could get the door open, I saw Jessie walking towards me. I said to myself, "Oh great, what poop was she going to stir up now" I was not in the mood for her. As she got closer, I could see her lips moving but had no idea what she was trying to say. I guess I looked confused or annoyed, so she started talking louder and appeared a bit shaken. I heard her say she had something important she needed to tell me. I thought maybe she was going to apologize for her behavior earlier at the family prayer, but I was about to be in for a big shock.

I rolled down my car window. Jessie grabbed both my hands. She started to cry so hard that I could barely understand what she was mumbling. I listened carefully and heard the words, "You were the last person your dad called before he died." Jessie said that she knew he had been on the phone right before he went outside and took his life. She wanted to know who he had called, so she talked to the phone company. BellSouth informed Jessie my home phone number was the last number dialed that morning. "I just wanted you to know that Patty." As I stood speechless (which was usually never) Jessie turned away from me and walked away. I sat silent against my car and tried to wrap my head around what I had just been told.

The ride back home to Marietta seemed like it took forever. I was so agitated and anxious that I could hardly sit still. I was in such a state of shock I just kept repeating "why did he call me?" "Why would I be the last person he called?" "Was he calling to tell me he was sorry for all the hurt he had caused or was he going to blame me for his problems?" I just said the same thing over and over. Carr, of course, was of absolutely no help. He looked over at me while I was talking out loud and said "What does it matter that he called you right before he offed himself? Dead was dead and I am thrilled he was gone."

Suddenly shifted thoughts and quietly began to wonder if this man I was sitting beside was the kind of person I wanted to spend the rest of my days with. The reoccurring theme of my life had just reared its' ugly head again. My dad had totally disappointed me by taking his life and never apologizing for all the pain he had caused. Now, my husband has completely disappointed me by not being there for me, either physically or emotionally. I saw the common theme playing out right in front of me again. The two men I should have been able to trust, respect and count on with all my being were both selfish, egotistical, self-centered people. One was out of my life forever and the other was inching his way towards the door, but neither of us knew our marriage was also headed to the graveyard.

CHAPTER THIRTEEN

The scribbled note I had written years ago started a healing process in my life, but as the years passed, I came to a place where I knew I had a lot more work to do in order for "contentment" to soak my body like a hot bubble bath. From this point forward, one would think the other things I will unpack would hold less significance in my process. That was not the case. So composing myself from the memories of my father's suicide, I dive back in. In this beaten up old relic of a suitcase, I find a Sunday Paper listing of all movies playing at Phipps Plaza on Sunday, September 21, 2003.

On the Sunday morning, I'm speaking of, I got up around 7:00am. As always, the first thing I did was to start a pot of coffee, and then went into the back sun room to watch the morning news. I always enjoyed the quietness of the house before Carr or the doggies got up. The doggies were my companions. We had two Airedales, Walter and Molly. They were adopted from the Airedale rescue group. Walter was the larger of these furry creatures. He had tan curly fur with black patches sprinkled around him. He was so docile and loving, but yet very loyal and protective. Thinking about Walter again makes me recall a funny story.

It was about 12 years ago, and we had a huge 60th birthday party at my home for Miss Shelly. My mom made some appetizers and sat the plate on the edge of my dining room table. She had prepared Ritz Crackers to compliment a cheddar cheese ball, rolled in almond slivers. When mom was out of the room, I looked over and saw Walter (who was about table height) reach up and snag an appetizer off of the platter. I hesitated for a moment, and then ran over and placed all the remaining crackers in neat rows so mom would not know something or someone had been eating her food before the party started. I had already been warned twice about touching the food before the guests arrived. I was starving but I knew better than to disobey my mom's orders. Even as an adult, the woman still scared me.

After the "appetizer" incident, my sister walked into the room and asked me what I had been giggling about. I told her about Walter and we both cracked up. My mom was not really a "dog" person. If she had any inkling Walter had taken food off of her appetizer plate, there would have been "you know what" to pay. Mom never knew about the cracker caper, until now. Boy, am I going to be in big trouble! That was such a great memory.

After enjoying my second cup of coffee, I drifted back to my childhood days and thought about how much going to church meant to me. I loved seeing all of my friends and the old gray haired ladies who gave you an evil eye if you misbehaved during the service. I even missed Mrs. Stafford with her bleached blonde beehive. We would stare at her as she sang in the choir. Her voice was so loud she would drown out everyone else. Once I passed her in the back hallway in our sanctuary and was looking closely at her bouffant. I remember her looking down at me and said "little girl always remember, the higher the hair, the closer to God." I will never forget moment or Mrs. Stafford's big hair. She must have owned stock in Aqua-net.

When I think if growing up and being in church every time the door opened, the memories are bittersweet. It was such a confusing time in my life. I would go into Sunday school, or R.A.'s and our lessons would be on God's love for us and how he would never forsake us or let us down. I felt so safe while in the haven of those church walls. But, when I would go home, the yelling, screaming, and beatings would start. I thought to myself "why doesn't God step in and help us?" or "why does God allow this man to go into the church and act all high and mighty, but go home and terrorize his family?" None of this made any sense to me. Maybe this was the reason I stopped going to church when I left home for college. I decided organized religion was no longer for me. I would honor God in my own "personal" way.

I am not really sure what I meant by, but could not bring myself to continue to go to church when I was forced to watch, for many years, this man who was beyond abusive, playing the part of the dutiful deacon and Christian father. I know I should not have judged him, but watching him put on this show week after week just made my stomach turn. I thought if this was going on in our home, what was going on in the homes of other members of our church: Do you really know anyone and does anyone really know what goes on behind closed doors?" I therefore, decided maybe church was not a "safe haven" as I had thought it was as a child and a teen. So, for now, I would sit in my large, lavish, and lonely home and finish my coffee.

About 9:00am, I heard Carr moving around upstairs. It sounded like he was getting dressed. When he came downstairs, he asked if we were still going to the movies. I told him I was looking in the Sunday paper as we spoke to see what movies were playing at Phipps. I kept looking down at the advertisement, but for some reason, I could not focus. I was feeling extremely anxious and was thinking to myself over and over again, "I do not want to go to a movie." I did not want to live with this man anymore and be responsible for his happiness. I am tired and beaten down. I am tired of thinking of things to do during the day, when he was home, because I did not want to be in the same room with him. He made my skin crawl when he got close to me.

Several weeks ago, Carr was in our bedroom petting and scratching Walter. I told him I wished he would massage my back like he did to the doggies. I needed a caress or just a touch, but instead, he looked right at me after I made these comments and said "the reason I scratch and rub on the dogs are they are soft and furry." What? Really? I could not believe what he had just said to me. Does that mean if I had a curly coat of fur, I could possibly be touched and massaged?

After 17 years of marriage, the reasons why I stayed no longer seemed like good enough reasons to keep staying. You see, the first few years after Carr and I were married, we were really happy and totally in love with one another. We did not have much money, but we were working hard towards making a better life for ourselves. I remember after we rented our small townhouse in the Dunwoody area, we purchased our first two big pieces of furniture. We bought a formal cherry dining room table, four chairs, and a big screen television from Macy's. We put these items on a revolving payment plan and paid about $40.00 per month until we got them paid off. We thought we were living "in tall cotton." As we say in the South.

The rest of our furniture, at the time, was either hand me downs from our parents, or a new piece here and there that we bought when we were single. Carr was 30 years old when we married, and I was 26. We both had been working and living on our own for several years, so, there were a few nice tables, lamps, bedding, etc., but mostly it was just some odds and ends. We were very proud of what we had. We did not have a lot of expensive material things at this point, but we had each other and that was all we needed to get by or so we thought.

Carr and I continued to work harder and harder and as a result, our standard of living got bigger and better. We bought several houses, and eventually ended up in the McLaren House. I traveled to London, Paris, Switzerland, Puerto Rico, and many more places. Carr had so many frequent flyer miles on Delta I never had to purchase a ticket. I always flew first class and stayed in the finest hotels. I drove a Porsche Boxster and had pretty much all the material trappings a person could want. However, I was probably one of the loneliest people on earth. Carr was never home, but on a rare occasion when he would make an appearance, most of his time was spent in his office working or on his computer doing who knows what.

I went on most of my trips either alone or with girlfriends. Carr never seemed to be able to get away to go with me. He showed no interest in me physically or emotionally. He had no interest in being intimate and we went years without being together as man and wife. It seemed the more we grew financially, the further we grew apart intimately. We had basically become roommates and our marriage had become one of convenience. We loved each other, but it was obvious, we were no longer in love. I did not know Carr anymore and certainly did not know myself. I no longer had an identity but was just known as Carr's wife.

My whole world seemed to revolve around Carr's wants, needs, and moods. I spent most of my days trying to keep his temperament from swinging too drastically. I worked so very hard to cover for him and was always making excuses for his behavior. I told friends and family he was just tired from traveling, or he was not feeling well. I had a story or excuse for just about any and everything.

Again, I was the consummate actress and knew how to play the part perfectly. The only downside to playing the "life was perfect role" was it takes a toll on the one who was working so hard to keep up the facade. I found I was exhausted and worn down. I was sick a lot, anxious all of the time, and walked on egg shells. I was always afraid if I did not keep Carr in a good mood, I would pay for it by either being verbally beaten down or just ignored.

When Carr would get in one of his "down" moods, it would take everything I had to try and pick him up. All of my time and energy was spent on trying to keep him from going to that dark place. Since I spent all of my strength and patience attempting to make Carr happy, I never really had time to try and figure out what I wanted or needed. I just blended into the woodwork of that old house.

During my sudden awakening, I realized my married life was eerily similar to my childhood. I was a door mat again and had no idea I had fallen back into the victim role. I really thought after my dad's death, I would be able to totally heal my battle wounds. I had left so much behind, but did not realize after severe trauma and long-term abuse, a person will usually go back to what was familiar and safe to them. That was why Carr was initially the perfect husband for me. He was belittling, degrading, and treated me like I was something he owned, not cherished. I had no idea I had put myself back into this familiar situation. About three years prior to the day I left my marriage; several life altering events took place and helped me make my final decision.

These events seemed to culminate at one time and started my realization I was having feelings of worthlessness and helplessness. I swore at my dad's funeral I would not let this happen to me again, but I had fallen right back into this comfortable, well known pattern. I decided to start counseling. It was evident I could not overcome my past until I completely dealt with my skeletons. Having to work through the pain, guilt, shame, and sadness was the beginning of the end of my marriage and made me look long and hard at myself, my choices, and my future. I truly hoped I would be leaving the role of victim behind once and for all.

I didn't know what to expect the first day I walked into the therapists' office. Yes, I had studied social work and psychology, but it was different when you are the one sitting on the couch pouring out your deepest, darkest emotions and vulnerabilities. As I looked around the office, I could see my therapist, Dr. Mary, had tried her best to make the space homey in a sterile sort of way. The walls were a painted light blue and the furniture was blue, red, green and khaki plaid. There were two end tables with large, outdated brass lamps on them. They were turned on and had very dim bulbs so as to keep the light from being too bright. Dr. Mary sat in a tufted, burgundy leather winged back chair. She sat straight up, looking straight at me with a notepad in her lap and a pen.

Dr. Mary began our first session by asking me "where I would like to begin." I responded I didn't know. I wasn't used to having anyone truly listen to me without judgment. Did I start with my adoption, or do I start at the deterioration of my marriage and then move backwards to the childhood stuff?

Although harder than I had imagined, I finally was able to say what I wanted and needed to say without getting beaten, slapped, ridiculed, or criticized. Maybe I thought perhaps someone would even value me and my feelings. I decided to start with my childhood. I hoped by doing this I would get to the core of some of my issues and maybe figure out why I kept repeating the same self destructive pattern over and over again. I refused to spend all of my days regretting decisions I have made and not ever knowing the person I was meant to be.

I was cynical about this whole therapy thing. I had never in my 42 years had anyone I could talk honestly too and I could trust. It seems all the people in my life so far have let me down and never met my expectations. Was there any kind, trustworthy folks in this world? If so, I hoped my new counselor was one of them. I sat back on the plaid couch, took a deep breath and asked Dr. Mary "so what do you want to know first?" She glanced over at me and said "what do you want me to know first?" I told her it was hard to find a starting place. I had so much to say, but the words are not going to come easy. Dr. Mary told me that was fine. She just sat and looked straight at me, crossed her legs and hands, and did not say another word. I realized it was going to be totally up to me to drive the conversation, so at this point, all I could say was "Here we go. You better sit tight Dr. Mary because this was going to be a very long and bumpy ride." She smiled at me and said "I am strapped in and ready to go."

I began my story around the time I was five years old, and my mom met the man of her dreams or so she thought. I told her about Kris and all of the abuse we endured while living with that man." I finally took a breath. I looked over and saw Dr. Mary had a very sad look on her face. She told me it would take a long time to work through the years or trauma and abuse, but it could be done. She told me we could get through it together. It was not going to be an easy road, but one could be overcome with honesty and mutual trust. I told her I was ready to get on the road to "true" healing.

I began to see Dr. Mary twice a week. In my sessions, we discussed the most painful memories, but also, made some of my most major life changing decisions. I had no idea how hard it was going to be to leave my old life behind. I had been married for seventeen years. I felt so alone and scared, but I had Dr. Mary, my mom and my sister in my corner. I had more love and support than many people and that was a blessing within itself. When I laid my head on my pillow each night, at night, I heard a little whisper in my ear saying "You can do it and I am here with you." Where was that voice coming from?

CHAPTER FOURTEEN

My suitcase is starting to look fairly empty and my load is becoming a bit lighter. I can finally begin to see the bottom of this, brittle old case. I think I feel a bit sad there are only a few items remaining. While unpacking, there has been a few times where I've felt a twinge of pity on myself for the past I have endured. But, pulling myself together and letting out a little giggle, I've come across some mortgage papers and a new hire packet.

After many counseling sessions and a lot of self discovery, I came to the see I was continuing to do things to sabotage myself and had to break the negative patterns I had learned as a child. I continued to repeat this negative behavior into my adult years and continued to make some very bad choices and mistakes. After starting my counseling with Dr. Mary, I had to take a hard look at my life and decide if I wanted to stay on this same destructive course, or if I wanted to work towards be content with my life. I made the decision I wanted the latter and worked very hard on beginning a new and positive chapter in my life. This was just the start of many new chapters out there just waiting for me.

In January of 2005, I purchased "my" very own home. It was an adorable three-story, putty-colored, cottage style home with a wrap around front porch. My home was located in a beautiful country club neighborhood in Cherokee County, Georgia. When you drove into the main gate of the community, all you could see was a perfectly manicured golf course, walkways lined with seasonal flowers, and lots of landscaping where men were working like little ants scurrying around here and there.

As you drove into the neighborhood, there were color coded sections in which the costs and sizes of the homes varied. My cottage was on Birchwood Lane which was in the blue zone. These were the smaller, less expensive homes which averaged in the $150,000 to $300,000 range. Just past the blue zone was the green zone. These were your typical 3,000 square feet homes which ranged from $300,000 to $500,000. The gold zone was the last zone and it was the furthermost from the front entrance. The homes in this area looked more like hotels and lodges and ranged from $500,000 to over $2,000,000. So technically, I was in the low rent district of the neighborhood, but was very proud of my little home. The mere fact it was my mine and mine alone was my source of pride. It was a calm, safe, peaceful haven. It felt so good to reach beyond my comfort zone and start doing things for myself instead of for everyone else.

After I up and moved to a different city, I still had to return to Marietta every now and then. Many of my doctors practiced there and I was not brave enough to start seeing a whole new crop of specialists. On my way home to Cherokee County, after an appointment with my Thyroid Specialist, I stopped by the local Kroger to pick up a few groceries. While, shopping, I had several folks come up to me and question me as to why I had moved out of my prestigious Victorian home. First of all, I could not figure out how these people I barely knew, had knowledge of my personal business and secondly, why did they care? Seeing how I really did not want to burn any bridges or hurt any feelings, I learned to just come up with some story about a job opportunity or something along those lines to appease them.

I, with Dr. Mary's help, had come to the realization I did not have to explain or justify why I had moved away, or my behavior in general. Really, who was going to believe what I had to say after I had been married to this manipulative, pitiful, and well-trained, liar. He had spun untrue stories of betrayal and despair all around town? I had made so many excuses, and protected his reputation for so long, my performance included the disguise of a perfect marriage. I knew I could not convince anyone this so-called kind, gentle, and loving man was really a self-centered, verbally abusive, narcissistic jerk. I had perpetuated this lie and did not have the energy to try and reverse the damage I had done.

I decided it was time to start with a clean slate. I bought my own home, a new car, and was hired at the Department of Family and Children Services (DFCS). I had taken my first steps towards becoming the person I am today and learning to love and respect myself for all I had to give to "me" and to others. I was learning to give out of love instead of guilt.

I started my job as a child protective services investigator on February 1, 2005. I had no idea what to expect from this new undertaking. I had not worked in a full time capacity in several years and had never worked as a paid social worker. On my first day at the Cherokee County Department of Family and Children Services (DFCS), I walked in the door and was shown my desk, in a small closet type room (similar to the one at Grady) that housed two other desks. I quickly met my supervisor, Toleesha, and she informed me I had a new investigation waiting for me on my desk and it required immediate attention. I looked around to see if she was talking to someone else, but quickly realized she was talking to me. It looked like the same kind of training I got at the start of my college internship and that would have been "none."

I walked into my new office and it did not take long to see there was not much room or privacy in this cramped space. There were two desks in this office along with files, notebooks, and much worn, stained child car seats lying everywhere. As I looked around, I did not know if I should laugh or cry. But there was no time for either of those. It was, once again, time to jump in feet first. I think it was called "baptism by fire." There was a paper clipped DFCS referral form on the center of my old gray metal desk that had appeared to have been painted many times. The top of the form listed the information on the mother of the child and was followed by the child's information. At the bottom of the referral was a written explanation of the allegations.

I sat down and began to read this document and could feel my emotions beginning to come to the surface and started to second guess myself again as to whether I could do this job or not. I started telling myself "you must focus on helping the kids and use what you know and have been through to make a difference." I repeated that in my head over and over again until I felt my blood pressure begin to come down and the redness of my face start to go away. Hopefully, if I could keep myself calm and focused. I really wanted to help in some small way. These kids deserved to know someone cared about them. I was going to do everything within my power to show them by a touch, a hug, or just listening to their fears and dreams. It was time for me to head out and start being the voice of children who have had no voice.

I completed the reading of the referral and headed out. I jumped into my sand colored Land Rover with a car seat under my left arm, and my file under the right. I opened the back door of my SUV and sat the car seat down and attempted to secure it with the seat belt. Then a very clear observation popped into my head. I had no idea how to strap one of these things into my car! I never had kids and my friends' car seats were always already locked into place. Even though I didn't know how to work this contraption, I refused to ask my co-workers for help. I didn't want to be laughed at or ridiculed. By some miracle I got the seat belt wrapped around the car seat. It looked fairly secure to me and deep down; I hoped a removal of the child was not going to be necessary. This would give me an opportunity to search the internet and find the proper way to secure a car seat before the secret was out.

As I cranked the car, I heard someone yelling my name from behind the vehicle. I turned and looked back and it was Jill. She was a seasoned investigator and had been assigned to mentor me and go with me on my referrals until she felt I was ready to tackle this job by myself. I was so happy to see her, but did not want to give away that I was a bit frightened about this new endeavor. Jill got in the front seat, asked to review the referral, and said, "Well, let's do it." I put the car in drive and we headed out to the Whispering Woods trailer park. I breathed a sigh of relief. Jill and I sat in the car heading towards the Holly Springs Exit off Interstate 575 and she started to give me a "mini lesson" on how to handle an investigation. She told me the first thing we needed to do was to contact the Cherokee County Sheriff's Department to escort us to the trailer since it was a methamphetamine related referral. After we contacted law enforcement, she said we need to make sure we reviewed the paperwork extensively so we could let the "client" know what the allegations were against them. After that was done, Jill said, "Then you fly by the seat of your pants, and always trust your gut feeling about the case and your surroundings. I smiled at her while she was on the phone talking to the dispatcher for the Sheriff's Department. She smiled back and we pulled into a red dirt turn-around at the entrance of Whispering Pines and waited for the deputies to arrive.

Once the police cruiser pulled up, we let down our window and gave the two deputies a briefing on the case and what we may possibly find at the residence. The deputies told us if they did locate drug paraphernalia, they would contact the GBI's narcotic team and have them take over the scene. As I listened to the plan, I thought "what in the hell have I gotten myself into?" It was my first day and I am already nervous about my safety. I decided to shake off my fear. Jill, the sheriff's deputies, and I all got out of our cars and headed to the front door of dilapidated white and rust colored metal home. The steps leading up to the small metal door, with a tiny star-shaped window on the front of it, were rotted and I did not know if they were going to fall in on us. After walking up the rickety, old steps, Jill and I stood in front of the door, and the deputies stood behind us so they could look in and see if there was anything that looked suspicious.

I proceeded to knock on this flimsy door and continued knocking for several minutes. We could hear someone in the house, but they had obviously decided not to answer. I am not sure if they saw the Deputies, but I would have assumed when law enforcement was knocking on your door, it was usually not good news. Especially if you are doing something in your residence that was dangerous and/or against the law. I knocked for a couple of minutes more and then Deputy Rose told me to step aside and he started to hit his fist on the door and tell the occupants they better open the door or he would obtain a warrant to enter. We then heard some scurrying going on inside and about two minutes later, the door opened and it was all I could do not to laugh out loud.

The woman who opened the door stood about six feet tall. She had on a crocheted bikini top, daisy dukes, and high heeled wedge sandals. She was extremely tan, had red hair with a blonde hairpiece attached to the top, and it appeared she had an Adams apple. I had never quite seen such a sight but kept telling myself I must treat all folks with respect and decency. About that time, I heard one of the deputies behind me whisper "I want her really bad." Well, of course, at that point I just could not longer hold in my laughter. As I began to giggle, I decided it was probably best I turn and walk away until I could pull myself together. So I decided to walk towards the car and act like I needed to get some paperwork out of the trunk. The deputies then proceeded to ask the woman if they could come in for a minute and look around. She hesitantly agreed. I walked back up those scary steps again and joined the group inside of the home. I would go over the referral while everyone else looked around. I was in no way prepared for what was going to unfold as the day went on.

I asked the woman what her name was and she said it was Shirley Campbell. I knew then I was speaking to the person who the allegations were against. I proceeded to ask her if she had a two-year old little girl named Tonya and she said she did. I asked where Tonya was right now and she said she was in her bedroom sleeping. Shirley appeared to be getting extremely nervous and I could see little sweat beads forming on her forehead. She began to get annoyed and asked what all of this was about in a very loud and harsh tone. I tried to remain, as calm as possible, and informed her that we had received a referral alleging a Meth lab was being operated out of her home. After I finished reading all of the allegations, I could see Shirley was angry and defensive.

Before Shirley could finish her ranting, I asked her if she would be willing to take a drug test. At that time, she shut down completely, refused the drug screen, and screamed for all of us to get out of her house. I Looked at Jill and both deputies and noticed they were heading towards the door. They waved for me to come and follow them out. So, I did and closed the flimsy door behind me. The four of us once again carefully negotiated the rotted steps and as we stepped down on the gravel driveway, we headed towards the police cruiser to discuss our findings. Deputy Rose said he was going to contact the narcotics unit and ask them to get a search warrant to search Shirley's home. He said he saw numerous butane torches, empty Sudafed wrappers, and several huge bags of fertilizer sitting in Tonya's room. I am guessing Shirley did not think anyone would peek into the little girl's room since she was sleeping. However, she was wrong and the rest of the day held some not too pleasant surprises for her and for that matter, me also.

While sitting in my car for hours waiting for the GBI to arrive with a search warrant, I felt like I was going to freeze to death. I had not dressed warmly enough for the day. I assumed I would be indoors most of the day. Boy was I wrong. It was frigid and unseasonably cold for January. Most southerners do not have the clothing necessary for extremely cold temperatures. I think to stay warm on this day; I would have needed to dress like an Eskimo preparing to build my igloo in the Alaskan Tundra. Instead, I had on a white Gap cotton turtleneck sweater, khaki pants, and a navy blue overcoat with checkered fleece lining. One would have thought this would have been sufficient, but in the cloudy, windy, rainy weather, it just was not enough.

On top of the waiting game in the cold miserable weather, I had removed Tonya from the house and she sat on my lap while we waited for the search warrant to get to the house. She had been a trooper for about an hour and a half but was now getting tired and irritable. I had not a clue about taking care of a toddler? If you remember, I did not even know how to strap in a car seat. This was getting a bit nerve racking and quite frankly, I was ready to be done with this day. As I began to daydream about a roaring fire and a glass of wine in my hand, I felt a warm sensation seeping through my khaki's. As I lifted Tonya off of my lap to see what was going on, I realized she had just peed all over my leg. I slowly moved her and placed her on the passenger seat next to me. I needed to come up with a plan as to what to do next.

I heard some commotion and laughter coming from the area where the sheriff's deputies and the guys who worked for the Criminal Investigation Division (CID). It dawned on me they were laughing at my reaction to the fact Tonya had peed all over me. At first, it kind of ticked me off to see these folks laughing at me, but I quickly started giggling too. It was really funny if you step back and took a look at the situation. I am sure my face reflected pure terror and if I saw someone else with that look, I would crack up too. As the laughter began to die down, a very handsome fellow came over and introduced himself as Detective David Jones. David said he was an investigator at CID and wanted to apologize if he had acted mean and hurt my feelings by laughing at my predicament. He then asked me if I wanted him to go to the neighbor's trailer (he knew the man living there because he had arrested him several times) and get a wet washcloth to clean my pants. I told him I would really appreciate that and off he went. When he came back with the washcloth, he helped me rub the pee off and then proceeded to sit in the passenger's seat and play with

Tonya and keep her occupied for a little while. David and I talked for about another hour.

David and I seemed to hit it off, but our chatting time was coming to an end. I saw the GBI's biohazard team pulling up in a truck and they had obtained the search warrant for the premises. As David got out of my car to go and brief the officers coming onto the scene, he looked and asked me if I would like to go out tonight and get a pizza. I thought for a moment and then blurted out "Sure!" He smiled and said "I will see you at eight o'clock for supper." I told him that would be great and off he walked. I decided to sit in the car for a few minutes and pull myself together. I did not know anything about going out on a date. I had been married to Carr for 17 years and had no idea what to say or do. What do you wear on your first date in almost twenty years?

I had been standing in the red clay and gravel front yard waiting for the opportunity to call the court for custody of this sweet little girl almost all day. I was hoping it would be soon so I could get warm and get out of these wet pants. I suddenly heard a tapping on my car window, so I rolled the window down. There stood Gary Watson, the head of the GBI narcotics unit, and he was requesting a briefing on my investigation and what action I would be taking in regards to the child. I told him that once I got confirmation that illegal drugs were being manufactured in this home, I would be calling the Juvenile Court and asking for State's Custody of Tonya. She would then be placed in a foster home. He thanked me, walked away towards the door of the trailer and just stood there in disgust, shaking his head back and forth. He seemed quite frustrated over the conditions in which this child had been living.

Gary then began to speak with his lead officer about the findings in the home. He proceeded into the trailer and the next thing I see was Shirley Campbell being escorted out of her home in handcuffs. I think I just got my clue as to what was found in the residence and I suspected it was more than just some run of the mill narcotics. It seemed as though Shirley was in big trouble. As I watched Shirley walking towards the police cruiser, I could see her red hairpiece had slid down from the top of her head and was resting on her shoulder. It was being held on by a few strands of bleached blonde hair. Instead of crying for Tonya and her sad existence, I laughed and found a way to add a little humor to the situation.

Once I pulled myself together, I called the court and was given custody of Tonya. I then called the office and notified the foster care division I needed a placement for this child. Tonya and I sat patiently in my car while her mother was transported to the local jail. About ten minutes later, my cell phone rang and I was notified a temporary home had been located. I jotted down the address and directions and Tonya and I headed towards her new home. As I dropped her off, I glanced down at my watch and realized I only had about an hour and a half to get ready for my date. I told the foster parents thank you for taking Tonya and I had to run.

I drove home quickly, showered, shaved my legs, dried my hair, and put on makeup with about ten minutes to spare. I was a little nervous, so I went down to the kitchen and got myself an ice cold beer. It tasted so good after such a long, crazy day. I drank it quickly. Then I realized the doorbell was ringing. The front door opened slowly as I pulled on the handle and slipped my left eye around the side of the door to make sure it was truly David. He was wearing a navy blue striped Rugby shirt, jeans, and brown loafers. He was a handsome "young" fellow with light brown hair, blue eyes, and a crew cut only a sergeant could be proud of. As I stood with the door open admiring his good looks, he asked me if he could come in. I cleared my throat and said, "Of course."

He wandered in, immediately took a seat on my beige damask sofa and propped his feet up on my round ottoman. I was a bit taken aback by his relaxed attitude and his making himself right at home. Maybe, I was the only one who was nervous since it had been over 18 years since my last date. It was hard to know how to act when you are so out of practice, but I decided to have another beer and get some liquid courage. David drank the beer I offered him, and I drank two more just to tame my nerves, and may I say, pretty much all of my butterflies were gone and I was ready to hit the road. We walked out my front door and I noticed he had driven his car from the sheriff's department. He told me. I would have to drive separately since it was against departmental policy for non-police personnel to ride in a county car.

As he was talking, I am thinking "Well, this was great. I have just had 3 beers and now I am going to drive." For some reason, this should have been my first clue as to how things were going to go, but being new in the dating arena, it just did not register. David backed out of my driveway and I followed close behind him. He went straight through the traffic light at the subdivision entrance and then immediately turned left into the parking lot where we had a Publix grocery store, a Mexican restaurant, a real estate office, and a small pizzeria named Vinnie's. He parked his car in front of Vinnie's, got out, and walked up to mine signaling for me to lower my window. As I did, he asked "Was pizza and beer okay?" "I thought to myself pizza would be good because it was fast, easy, and we won't be here half of the night."

As sad as it seems, I was a working woman in my early forties and my bedtime was very important to me. If I did not get my sleep, I become a raging maniac. There are not too many people I work with who would want to spend time with me in that state of grumpiness. So, pizza would be just the ticket. I told him that was fine, got out of my car, and headed into Vinnie's on my first official date since divorcing Carr.

The owner of the restaurant came over and seemed to know David well. He shook his hand and asked who this lovely lady with him. He told the owner that we worked together and we were coming in for some good pizza after a very long day. After David introduced me, I did not know how to take his comment. Were we just work acquaintances having some supper, or were we on a date and enjoying each others' company? This was going to have to be answered soon or I will be home, in my bed (alone, for those of you whose minds go to the gutter quickly...) earlier than I originally thought. The waiter came to our booth and asked us what we wanted to drink. David said he would have water since he was in a county car but for me to order what I wanted. I ordered a Diet Coke and he and I proceeded to chat with just some small talk as we looked at our menus. I have to say I felt a bit uneasy and this was compounded when David told me, "Now, you can order anything you want and if you want several toppings on your pizza that was okay too."

I could not believe what he was saying. I mean we are at a pizza place for gosh sakes. It's not like we were at Chop's or a restaurant of that caliber. Did I hear him correctly? I could buy this restaurant if I wanted to and I was being told I could order more than one topping for my pizza! Are you kidding me? After I talked myself off of the building, I decided I needed to chill and at least give him a chance. Maybe I did not fully understand what he said, and was rushing too quickly to judgment. So, I took a deep breath, regrouped and decided to give him another chance.

After we ordered an extra large New York special, David asked about my past relationships and we began to discuss our histories. I told him I had been divorced for a couple of years and had been married for 17 years. He appeared to be very sincere and caring in his responses and that made me feel a bit more comfortable. David then told me about a girl he had dated and lived with for over 3 years and their recent breakup. We talked about being hurt, and how things that once were so right can turn so very wrong. I listened as he talked, and could hear the sadness in his voice. As he talked more his sadness seemed to be turning to anger and I was once again feeling uneasy.

As he described their break up, it almost seemed as if he had been stalking her. I did not like what I was hearing. My comfort level was dropping rapidly and I was trying to figure out how to bow out of this date gracefully. I continued to plot as he talked. He had been in a special operations unit in the army and had been all over the world on undercover missions. He lifted his shirt and told me to look at his tattoo. It was some type of warrior eagle. Just as I thought I could not get grossed out any further, he began telling me about his pet boa constrictor. Now, I knew I had to come up with a reason to get the hell out of there.

Not only did I despise snakes, but when the ferrets were mentioned, that was it. I slowly arose from the table, excused myself and went to the ladies room. I stayed in there for about five minutes. I returned to our table and told David I was not feeling well and needed to go home. It had been such a long day and I was probably just tired from all of the drama at the Meth lab. He said he totally understood and asked if he could follow me home to make sure I got there safely. I explained that he was very kind, but I would be fine. I thanked him for a nice evening, turned, walked out the front door, got in my car, and vowed never to go on a date again. That night, I discovered all of the disastrous, nightmare dating stories my friends have told me about were true.

I walked into the office on Monday morning and Jill rushed up to me wanting to know how my date went. She was so bright-eyed and bushy-tailed I hated to burst her bubble. Yet, I proceeded anyways to give her the run down on the evening. She was disappointed things did not go better, but she started laughing out loud and told me she would have given anything to see the look on my face when David told me about the snake. After we shared a good laugh about the reptile and the permission to order whatever I would like from the menu, we gave each other and big hug and went back to our respective offices to see what the day would have in store for us.

The two years I spent as an investigator for DFCS were difficult, sad, stressful, and at times gut wrenching, but on the upside, I made some great friends. When you share the experiences of abuse, molestation, and just plain old evil with a group of people day in and day out, a bond forms that can never be broken. We laughed and cried together. There were marriages, break-ups, and even a couple of affairs that took place. We supported each other no matter what and for those moments of friendship, that no one could understand unless they had shared our experiences, I am forever grateful. This group of women helped me on the road to having confidence in myself and knowing I am a kind, intelligent, self-sufficient person who can overcome the abuse and degradation. The lessons I learned about myself and others will be with me forever, and hold a special place in my heart.

CHAPTER FIFTEEN

I'm suddenly realizing my back is aching so badly I need to sit up for a few minutes and stretch it out. I have been leaning over this suitcase for hours on end and so engrossed in the thoughts and memories, I am just now noticing the light is beginning to peek through my wooden shutters. It's morning. I have been unpacking all night long and oblivious to the time, but was now aware of it along with the fact I am in pain, both physically and emotionally. Maybe it's time to stop for a while. No, I need to get through this and giving up is not an option. I am getting up, stretching, taking some Advil and its back to the floor for me. I'm down to the bottom of the case and only see four or five things still lying there waiting to be taken out.

I dig down inside and pull out a DVD. It's a movie that holds a special place in my heart. The movie is *Walk the Line* which is the love story between Johnny Cash and June Carter. When I began to watch this movie one Friday evening, I had no idea this would be the beginning of another special love story.

After two long, but incredibly insightful years working at DFCS, I decided it was time to move back to Marietta. I needed to face the demons I had been running away from. There were so many people I thought were close friends and whom I trusted, but once the divorce was final and Carr started spinning his tales, I realized during the time of illness, financial woes or divorce, you truly find out who your friends are.

Since Carr and I had so many mutual friends, I had made a promise to myself I would not expose or air our dirty laundry in public. I would not try and "win" them as my exclusive friends. I told myself I would take the high road but from what I could tell, Carr decided not to take that path. He wanted revenge on me for "walking out on him." Of course, I had no idea of the extent of campaigning and trash talk Carr perpetuated. To my shock and disbelief, I began noticing certain friends were not returning my calls or emails. I heard rumors, which were clearly not true, about me and my family in local stores and restaurants. Being deemed an outcast from the community which I had so loved and gave back to was just more than I could bear. At night, when I would try and fall asleep, I would curl up in a fetal position and cry so hard I would soak my pajamas and my pillow,

Since I had felt so betrayed, I decided it would be best for me to move away from this town and get my life together and that was exactly what I did. For over two years, I left my old life and began to work on building a new one for myself. As I began to get stronger, I started coming to the clear realization a lot of people were never true friends. It was time to leave them behind for good. I had made so many awesome friends through work, tennis and my neighborhood, I discovered it was becoming very easy to say goodbye to many from my past and cherish those in the present.

I found a house in Marietta that I immediately fell in love with and it was for sale. It sat on John Ward Road, which was about 3 miles west of the Marietta

Square. The house sat back off the road quite a bit and resembled a country farmhouse. It was an all white, one level home with a huge wrap around rocking chair front porch. There was a two car attached garage and another three-car detached garage that could be used for a workshop. The back yard was about a third of an acre and was fenced in with a doggie door leading into the attached garage. I had gotten a medium sized, golden, fury mutt at the Cherokee County animal shelter and named her Penny. Since I would be working all day, the doggie door was perfect as Penny would definitely need her own access to the outdoors.

I put an offer on the Marietta house, put my cottage, in Bridgemill up for sale, and was made an offer from the Cobb County State Court for a position as a probation officer. Things were looking up for sure. All these new beginnings, but still, I had not really dated anyone more than a couple of times, and really did not want to. I was by no means ready to get into a relationship. I had too much going on and did not have time for men! My offer on the Marietta house was accepted and my cottage had a contract on it. I accepted the position at the Cobb County State Court and promptly put my resignation in at DFCS. In January of 2006, I hired a moving company and headed back home. I must say, it felt really good to be back in the town I loved with my feet firmly planted and my head held high.

After digging through boxes, boxes, and more boxes, I finally found a pair of black pants I could wear on my first day of work at the probation office. I was very nervous. There were a lot of changes going on in my life and it was difficult to slow down and put each new experience in perspective. Everything was kind of a blur, but I knew eventually things would settle down and life would have some sort of normalcy and balance. But for now, I was just flying by the seat of my pants and trying to enjoy the ride.

Monday arrived. I got up, had my morning coffee in my new kitchen, got dressed in my new bedroom, got into my new black BMW and drove to the courthouse for the first day of my new job. I parked in the employee deck and walked around the building. It was sort of bittersweet walking up the same sidewalk where Carr and I would take our Airedales, Walter and Molly for long walks. With some sadness in my heart, I had to focus on the task at hand and try to figure out which door I go into to get to my office. I saw a deputy standing out front of the courthouse in his brown polyester shirt and pants and decided to ask for help. As I approached him, he began to smile and asked if he could help me. I told him of my dilemma and he kindly told me, until I had a court badge, I could not enter the building through the employee's entrance, I had to enter at the front and go through court security.

I thanked him, walked quickly in the front door and proceeded to go through the metal detectors. I successfully got through the security line and walked around the corner into the State Probation Office. I went in, told the receptionist who I was, and she buzzed me back. I was taken back to Fred Barker's office, and told to have a seat. As Fred entered, he introduced himself as the Chief Probation Officer and welcomed me to his team. Fred appeared to be a rather quirky fellow, and he really reminded me of Barney Fife. My saving grace was the knowledge I would only have to deal with this odd, wimpy man on a limited basis. I felt that would be tolerable.

While sitting in Fred's office, a short, cranky, older woman with a gray bob haircut came in and introduced herself as Beverly Chilton. She said she was my supervisor and if I would follow her, she would take me to my work station. As we arrived at my 5' x 5' cubicle, she went over my job description, and my case load. She seemed to be a very genuine, hard working woman. First impressions are not always what they appear and neither was Beverly. But for now, I was off to a great start. I began looking over the paperwork left for me on my desk and realized that this particular probation office handled misdemeanor cases such as DUI's, minor drug possession offenses, traffic violations, and park perverts. My case load was about 480 cases with over 200 that reported to me on a monthly basis. I put my head down and dug in with both feet.

As the weeks went by and I started to feel more comfortable with my job and my co-workers, I slowly branched out and made a couple of new friends. One person in particular would turn out to be a very special friend. Madeline Weiss, had worked in the probation department for many years and was always willing to help with questions or just as a sounding board. She had a large office and I would go in and sit in the mornings when we both arrived a little early. In her office, we would catch one another up from the happenings of the previous day. We started going to lunch and became closer as the days passed. There was a group of four of us who got along well and enjoyed doing things together. The only problem was my supervisor did not like the other three women I was hanging out with, and my life was beginning to get extremely difficult as a result of this friendship. The stress and tension got so bad, after about a year of constant negativity and verbal battering from Beverly, I finally resigned. Of course, Fred was of no help as he played both ends against the middle did not have the balls to stand up and lead the department. Such poor leadership was of no use to me and the others who went before me.

There was one awesome thing that came out of my brief stay at the probation department. One random Friday, Madeline and I had gone to grab a bite of lunch before we both had to be back for court. As we were driving to the restaurant, she suddenly blurted out the name Jake Hart. "I have got to introduce you to Jake! You guys would be perfect together." I sat perfectly still in my seat. It has been over two years since I had a "real" date and just did not know how I felt about branching out again. Between the Meth lab detective and a blind date that had a blonde highlighted mullet and drove a truck with flames air brushed down the side, I just did not know if I had the strength to get back up on that horse and ride.

Madeline began telling me about this Jake guy. I gave it a brief thought and told Madeline that maybe when I got back from a long planned vacation to Thailand, I may consider going out with him. I told her to let me know if he ever wants to get together and we can possibly set something up. I really did not think much about it over the next few months. Two weeks passed since Madeline told me about Jake, and before I knew it, it was time to leave for trip. In Thailand, my tennis buddies and I had an awesome time and returned with pictures and stories to last a lifetime. It was a trip I will never forget, but it was time to return to work and get back to reality. After returning from my journey, life in general was fairly mundane and consisted of going to work, playing tennis and hanging out with family and friends on the weekends.

August 5, 2006, was just another mundane work day until Madeline called me into her office. She said her husband, Jake Weiss, had just called and wanted to know if I was interested in coming to their home that evening to meet Jake. I asked Madeline why she called both Jake's by their first and last name. She said both Jake's had grown up next door to each other in Powder Springs and was the only way they could keep each other straight. I laughed and told her a cookout at her house sounded just great and I would not mind meeting a new friend but wanted nothing more.

Madeline called Jake Weiss and told him it was a go. We decided to meet at the Weiss' house at 7:00pm that evening. I rushed to get home from work so I could shower, dress, put on make-up, and get to the Weiss' house on time. I was nervous about the whole blind date thing, especially after boa constrictor boy and mullet man. But what the heck, I thought, what was one night of my life?

I got home, put on a denim skirt, a white t-shirt and black slides. I was happy that a little bit of my tan from Thailand was still intact and I would not look like a tourist who had just arrived from Canada. All in all, I looked pretty good and was looking forward to some quality social time with Madeline, if nothing else. I pulled into Jake and Madeline's driveway and saw an older model green Honda Accord and a newer Honda Accord parked under the carport. I suddenly realized I had some major butterflies swirling around in my tummy. Maybe I could pretend I had the flu and go back home. *"No, Patty,"* I told myself, Get *out of that car and march your butt up to that door*! And that was exactly what I did with knees and hands shaking. I knocked on the door and was extremely happy to see Madeline's smiling face welcoming me to her home.

This was the first time I had been to the Weiss' home, and of course, the first thing I wanted to know was the location of the bathroom. Madeline pointed towards the hallway and told me it was the first door on the left. As started to walk through the kitchen, down the hall towards the bathroom, I saw a nice looking fella sitting in a chair at the kitchen table and thought to myself *Well, maybe this evening will not be so bad after all.* He had jet black hair, green eyes, a very handsome face, and a beautiful smile that lit up the room. When I walked by him, he stood up and introduced himself as Jake Hart. He then asked me if I would like a frozen margarita. According to him, his margaritas were famous and I certainly needed to try one. I told him maybe I would have one when I got out of the bathroom.

I proceeded down the hall and he sat back down in the chair in the kitchen. While in the bathroom, I could hear him laughing and it was so contagious. I really began to look forward to the evening. I think we were going to have a good time and I was always up for a good margarita. When I walked back into the kitchen, I looked right at Jake and asked, "Well, where is my margarita? Have you just been sitting there the whole time I have been gone?" He got a big smile on his face, got up and made me one delicious drink. For the next hour or so, the four of us sat and talked, laughed and got to know one another a bit better. Jake told me he had been in the midst of a nasty divorce for the last several years and had four-year old twins, Nat and Jakey. As I was trying to wrap my head around all of that, he told me his kids were living with his dad and stepmom. His soon-to-be ex-wife, Andrea, had made false allegations of abuse against him, and DFCS had removed the kids in order to investigate. The kids had been out of his custody for the past eight months. Unfortunately, Andrea had previously worked in a mental health facility while attending college, so she had first-hand knowledge of how DFCS worked. She knew if she made allegations of sexual abuse, they would have to be thoroughly investigated. She also knew it was very difficult to disprove abuse had taken place.

This whole mess had turned out to be a mental and financial nightmare for Jake, but he was doing all he could to hold it together. He was fighting with every bone in his body to get custody of his kids and get them out of this horrible nightmare. As Jake continued to tell his story, I could see the heart-wrenching effect all this was having on him. I was impressed with how he had conducted himself thus far. It takes a very strong person to get through something like that without lashing out in anger or trying to destroy the other person. From what I could tell, he had neither lashed out at Andrea nor tried to make her life a living hell. This amazed me and I wanted to know more about this man.

After talking for about thirty more minutes, we decided to move into the den and watch a movie about Johnny Cash's life titled *Walk the Line*. Jake and Madeline sat on one denim sofa and Jake and I sat on the other. He was about a foot away from me on the sofa, and quite frankly, it did not bother me at all. I liked having him close and I think I leaned in a little so we would be closer. The movie started and I was totally content. About forty minutes into the movie, I could feel my nose starting to get stuffy and my eyes were starting to itch and swell. This could not be happening! I was having an allergic reaction to something! I asked Madeline if they had pets and she told me she had three cats. I'm highly allergic to cats, and according to Jake Weiss, the cats sleep on these two couches all of the time. At that point, my nose was totally closed and I could feel my throat swelling. This was not good!

I jumped off of the couch and said my goodbyes. I was literally running out the door so I could get home and take some Benadryl. I needed to reduce the swelling and open up my nose and throat. On the way to my car, I heard someone calling my name. When I turned around, Jake was running after me trying to say goodbye and let me know he had a good time. I jumped in my car, lowered the window, stuck my head out and told him, "I had a good time too." As I drove away, I figured I would never hear from Jake again after such a fiasco.

I got home, took some allergy medicine and went to bed. It had been a really long day.

Monday rolled around and the first thing I did when I arrived at work was to go into Madeline's office to explain to her why I left in such a hurry. I walked in and she sat behind her desk with a goofy smile on her face. I asked her, "What are you grinning about?" She looked right at me and told me, "Jake said he really enjoyed meeting you and you seemed like a really nice girl. He also wanted to know if it would be okay if he called you when he gets back from his trip." I let Madeline know I would like that a lot. I walked out of her office, headed to my cubicle with a huge grin on my face, and knew it was going to be a good day.

It was about a week after Jake and I first met when I got a call from him asking me if I would like to go out Saturday evening. Since he flew for a major airline, his schedule was fairly erratic so it was hard for him to plan too far ahead. He was currently flying a lot of overtime. He needed the extra money to cover his legal bills while fighting for custody of his children. Once again, I really respected the fact he was working so hard to do the right thing for his kids and trying to get them out of the hell on earth they were living in. I said I would love to see him again and we agreed we would get together Saturday. I hung up the phone and realized my tummy was swirling again. It had been a long, long time since a guy had given me butterflies.

Saturday came around and I spent the morning trying to figure out what I would wear for my date that evening. *Do I wear a sundress? Some nice shorts and a tee shirt? Or a jean skirt?* It was really hard to decide but I finally put on jeans, a black shirt, and black sandals. This was cute, but also, casual. I did not want to look too dressed up and have him get the idea I expected him to take me somewhere expensive. I knew things were tough for him financially at this time. He was paying child support, a house payment, and paying attorneys' fees out the booty. I just wanted to spend some time with him and hear his infectious laugh again. His smile made my heart feel warm and secure. I was glad I was going to see him in a few hours.

About 7:00pm, I heard a car pull into my driveway. I looked out of the den window and saw Jake. My heart began racing and my palms felt sweaty. *What the heck was wrong with me! I thought to myself. I am a grown woman and I am feeling like a young school girl waiting by the door for her first date!* This was just crazy, but it was a good crazy. I walked to the front door and waited for him to come around the corner. When he saw me waiting at the door for him, he got that really big smile and gave me a little hug. We walked into the family room and he proceeded to tell me how nice I looked. It was such a good feeling to be complimented by a man. For most of my marriage, I don't think Carr knew or even cared that I needed to be seen, acknowledged and shown some attention. It was nice to be hugged and touched by a man. To have fun and be able to act silly without being chastised or demeaned. I think I was going to have to relearn how to have a good time and how to be myself. When you have played a role for over 40 years and have not been authentic, it was so very hard to reach deep inside and find the true person stuffed down deep in my body. But for now, I was going to enjoy the smiles, laughter and Jake's kindness.

The evening went well and we decided we would hang out together the next day. I told him if he wanted to come for dinner, I could make a big pot of spaghetti and we could eat, and try and watch the rest of the movie we attempted to watch on our first date. He laughed and said that sounded great. We agreed on a time and off he went. At the time, Jake was living in an older, brick ranch home in Lithia Springs which he had bought from his dad. He was living there while he renovated the house. He wanted to rent the home out and buy something for himself once he figured out where the kids would be living and how much space he would need. It took him about 45 minutes to drive to my home, but he let me know I was worth the drive.

Having someone say nice things to me and treat me with respect felt unusual and a little uncomfortable. How does one take down the walls that had been put up for survival and let someone in to that very private and guarded world? It was frightening. I was going to have to step out of my comfort zone and allow someone to be nice to me. Between my dad, my ex-husband, and old friends who dropped me like a hot potato after my divorce, I did not have a good track record for bringing people in my life that were, loyal, honest and trustworthy. How was I going to reach out and accept this precious gift I had been offered? I did not have the answer, but knew I was going to try very hard not to push him away. I was going to give this a shot, but I will go in with my eyes wide open, and my heart well guarded.

Jake and I began to see each other on his days off. We did just about everything together and we were having a ball. We went glider flying, hiking, to movies, dinners and he would meet me for lunch on a regular basis. He made me laugh and this was something I needed to do so badly. At a time of great stress and turmoil, he continued to be kind, gentle, and did not seek revenge or harbor hate. I had been so used to Carr being angry all of the time, for basically no reason at all. I exerted every ounce of energy trying to keep him balanced. While Jake was dealing with an uncertain future and the possible loss of his children, he somehow continued to be a loving and caring person. He took the high road and loved hard with everything he had. I saw myself slowly beginning to open up to him and let him get a little glimpse of my heart. It had gotten hard from the abuse, stress and heartache I had suffered throughout my past, but I could feel it getting a tiny bit softer. It was such a good feeling and I hoped as time went by, it would soften a little bit more.

In October of 2006, Jake rented out his house in Lithia Springs and had no place to live. He could not go and stay with dad since his kids were living there. He could not afford much rent since he was currently paying a mortgage, child support, and paying his step-mother over a thousand dollars a month to take care of his kids. After all his debts were paid, there was not much left over for him. I thought long and hard and decided he could move in with me for the short term. I had plenty of room and he was pretty much living with me anyway. He took me up on my offer and moved in to my home in Marietta. I had to say I liked having him there with me. He made me feel safe and made my house feel more like a home.

As Jake and I went about our daily lives, he continued going to court on a monthly basis and saw his kids once a week for two hours. The kids would come to my house and we would visit with them. Since they were in the State's custody, there had to be a person supervising our visits. This was so surreal. I used to supervise parental visits and now I am the one being supervised. It really made Jake and I both angry that here we were professional, well-educated people being put into the middle of this custody mess. The only choice was to wait patiently and let things fall into place in God's time.

Speaking of God's time, Jake asked me if I would like to join him on Sunday morning for church. I told him that sounded good, but was nervous about stepping into a place of worship. I had not walked into a church since my dad's funeral. The very thought of going into a church with all of those people, who were possibly big time hypocrites, made me sick to my stomach, but I agreed. We decided to go to church with Jake's dad and step-mom. That way, we could see the kids with the State's approval (of course). Jake and I walked down the church isle in this very large sanctuary holding hands. There was a special feeling being back in a church. I deeply felt a sense of being home. As he and I sat down and got comfy, several people came up and welcomed us. This was so reminiscent of the men, women, and children I grew up with at Beulah Baptist Church. I liked the warm, settled feeling I was experiencing and realized some of my happier memories were coming back and I could feel a smile on my face. I must say it was good to be back in God's House.

October and November passed by quickly and Jake and I worked, hung out on Saturday's and went to church together on Sunday's. We had settled into a routine and we realized we enjoyed being together and both of us wanted this relationship to continue. Just as things had finally calmed down for both of us, bam! We got hit with a new issue: Jake's dad and step-mom decided, at the end of December, they could no longer take care of the kids. They contacted DFCS and told them they would need to find the kids a new home no later than December 29th.

I am making an assumption, but I do think the case manager, Mrs. Greene, thought the grandparents would keep the kids a bit longer. Jake and I thought the grandparents would reconsider since DFCS had no foster homes in which to put the kids. December 29th arrived and the grandparents called DFCS and told them to come and get Jakey and Nat. Their stuff was packed and waiting at their front door.

Around noon on Friday, I received a call from Mrs. Greene. I had worked with her briefly when I was employed with DFCS and she had transferred to the Bartow County office from the Cherokee County office since Jake and Andrea were residents of Bartow County at the time the children were removed, the county retained jurisdiction. Mrs. Greene was in a tizzy and asked me if there was any way I could take the kids for a few months while she located a suitable foster home. If I could not take them, they would be sent to a group home. I could not believe what I had been hearing. A group home? Really? Why would grandparents throw Jake's kids out on the street after they had adopted their grandchild when she was two years old? Why was it okay for them to adopt her, but hang these children out to dry? I was, for a brief moment, speechless. I asked Mrs. Greene what I needed to do and she told me I would have to have a background check, a drug screen, and have a case manager come and approve my home. I thought *what choice do I really have? I cannot let these kids go to a group shelter*. I agreed to do it for a short period of time. What did I know about kids? I had been childless my entire life and had absolutely no idea how to take care of kids, and these were 4 year-old twins who had never been told "no" a day in their lives. Oh Lawd, what had I gotten myself into now!

I left work around 2:00 on that memorable Friday afternoon and was fingerprinted at the Sheriff's office, drug screened, and drove home to get ready for my home evaluation. By 5:00pm, I had been approved and was given the all clear to go and pick the kids up at their grandparent's home. Jake got permission to go with me and off we went. We got to the house in Douglas County and both kids were waiting at the front door with all of their belongings. I did not know whether to laugh or cry. This was definitely an unexpected turn in my life. We loaded my car with clothes, games, bikes, skateboards, and headed for Marietta. On the hour drive to my house, I just kept thinking *what am I going to do with two kids to take care of? What do they eat? What if I don't like them? When do they go to bed? Do I read them a story?* These questions played over and over in my mind. About twenty minutes later, I pulled myself together. I thought *if some people I had seen parenting can do it, then so can I.*

As we pulled down my driveway, Jakey asked his dad if he was going to be living with Miss Patty. His dad told him yes. Jakey did not say much after that. It was pitiful. These kids had moved several times since being removed by the State and Jakey always looked so sad. I tried to lighten the mood just a little, but soon realized these children did not feel like being jovial. I felt my heart aching for these two little people. The four of us walked in my garage door and into the family room. There was a pool table in this room and both kids ran to it and started rolling the balls from side to side. They seemed to be having fun and I started to loosen up just a bit. As they played with the pool balls, Jake and I unloaded their belongings and put them in the back bedroom next to mine. Jakey would not sleep in a bed by himself since being taken away from his parents. I think sleeping in the room with his sister made him feel a little more secure.

When the kids were removed from their mother, they were put in separate foster homes for several days. To separate siblings was bad enough, but to separate twins was just unthinkable. Since that day, Jakey and Nat both would not sleep without one another. They had been traumatized tremendously. What was letting them sleep in the same room going to hurt. Nat would sleep in the queen-sized bed and Jakey would sleep on a blow up mattress on the floor. He loved it because he was, "floor camping." About 8:00pm, Jake told me it was time for him to go. He would be staying at his dad and step-mother's home while the kids were living with me. He had to play musical chairs once again, as far as, living arrangements go. With huge tears in his eyes, he kissed his kids goodbye. They hugged him and cried which made him cry even harder. It was gut wrenching to see this exchange. These kids and their dad were being put through hell for no reason except Andrea hated Jake more than she loved her kids. Andrea had been abandoned as a child by her mother. She had some major junk she had never dealt with. This junk was now being directed towards her husband and children. I knew the pain of childhood trauma, but I also knew if you did not deal with it on some level, it would deal with you. Her demons were surfacing and destroying this family.

Eventually, the kids let go of their dad and Jake left. Both Nat and Jakey were still crying after the front door was closed. I looked at these little people and thought *what am I supposed to do now?* Luckily, the next day was a Saturday so I did not have to go to work. This would give me time to get acclimated to my new situation and hopefully, get the kids settled down before they started yet another preschool on Monday. I decided since we were all tired from such an emotional day, maybe we should all get in the queen sized bed and watch a movie. I dug through their bags and found "The 12 Dogs of Christmas." I put the DVD in, and about 30 minutes later, all three of us were sound asleep and did not wake until 7:00 the following morning.

We all got up and I went into the kitchen to make my morning coffee. About the time I sat down on the couch for my first cup of caffeine, Jakey came running in and asked "Can we watch cartoons?" I looked at him with a blank stare and said "Cartoons?" He told me it was Saturday morning and they always watched cartoons on Saturday morning. I said "sure" and the three of us watched Tom and Jerry for about an hour. Once my cartoon tolerance level had been reached, I got up and went back into my room and watched the news. Thirty or so minutes after I began watching the news, Nat comes in and tells me she and Jakey are hungry. I was so out of my element, I had not even thought of what we were going to eat for breakfast. Jake and I had purchased groceries the week before, but I did not have kid's cereal, pop tarts and stuff like. I had to improvise and we had peanut butter and jelly sandwiches. The kids loved having sandwiches for breakfast, and it was something quick and easy to fix. The first meal was done and we had the whole day to hang out. *What was I going to do with two kids all weekend?* This was going to be a challenge, but I liked a good test.

After several movies, bike riding, walks to the playground and thrown together meals, Monday finally arrived. Around 6:00am, I woke the kids up and got them dressed and fed. I put them in front of the television while I got ready for work. I grabbed a breakfast bar, got everybody belted in the car, and off we went to preschool. I got everyone out of the car at the school, walked both of them inside, and all three of us cried when I left. I cried all the way to work, which took me about ten minutes. I did not know if I was crying for the children or crying for myself. I think it was a combination of both. It broke my heart to leave them at the day care center all day. They had been left by so many people, and I wanted to let them know I was there for them. These kids needed some stability in their lives and I would do everything in my power to see they got it from me and their dad.

The first few weeks, the three of us spent each day developing a routine. By the end of the third week, we were fairly settled and things were going well. The fourth week, things began to go downhill. I was receiving about five phone calls a day from the DFCS case manager wanting to know where the kids were and asked all kinds of ridiculous questions. It was very hard for me to try and answer these questions, especially with my job. I saw defendants each day, and had court several times a week. It was impossible for me to answer these harassing phone calls multiple times a day. My supervisor called me into her office and asked what was going on. When I told her, she let me know under no uncertain terms these calls had to stop. I passed this on to the case manager, Mrs. Greene. She told me Andrea was calling her office all day long stating the kids were not at preschool and had not been there for days. I knew this was a load of crap, but unfortunately, the case manager had to follow up on all accusations. Mrs. Greene made it very clear she had no choice but to make sure the kids were where they were supposed to be. I knew this was going to turn into a huge problem. It did.

Six weeks or so after I got the kids, a permanent foster home was found for them. The foster home was about five minutes from my house. I hated I could no longer keep them with me, but I could not afford to lose my job.

I did not know how I was going to tell them they were moving again. This whole mess infuriated me. This woman was once again contributing to the trauma these kids were experiencing. They did not understand why they could not stay with me. If you had ever tried to explain the concept of mental illness to a four-year-old, let me tell you, it was not easy. Jake and I told them, "Mommy's brain was not working right and the judge does not think it was a good idea for them to see her right now." This appeased them for a bit, but Jake and I knew the harder questions would come later. We were also slightly afraid Andrea would be given joint custody. If this happened, life was going to get even more difficult. I just did not know how much more these kids could take emotionally. They were strong little people, but everyone has a breaking point.

It was the beginning of March and we reluctantly packed the kids belongings and took them to their new foster home. As we drove up the long, winding driveway, I could not believe my eyes. We pulled up to an enormous brick three story home. I jokingly thought to myself *maybe I could move in too*. We knocked on the huge stained glass front doors, and suddenly a feeling of calm came over me. I knew we had angels there with us and the kids were going to be just fine.

As the door opened, out walked a man and woman, probably 40ish, with the sweetest smiles. They welcomed us in and introduced themselves as Pam and Craig Williamson. We went inside and I was admiring their home when several kids came sliding down a circular pole. Pam and Craig had four kids Anna, Charles, Noel and Christie. Their ages were 6, 11, 12, and 16. The older of the children, Christie, was at soccer practice. She did not spend much time at home anymore. The kids were sent to play and Pam, Craig, Jake and I all sat down in their dining room and began getting to know each other. Pam and Craig told us they were foster parents for a private agency and only took a couple of kids into their home each year. When they heard about Nat and Jakey, and what they had been through, they told the agency they would be more than happy to foster them until custody had been decided. Jake and I felt at ease, hugged the kids while they cried, and drove down the long, tree lined driveway, both crying and hurting for his children.

As the months passed, the kids got settled in their new home, and the court hearings continued. Jake and I became much closer through all the trials and tribulations. When we slowed down long enough to take a deep breath, we realized we had fallen in love. We were so immersed in this whole custody and divorce mess; we had not taken an inventory of our feelings. We knew we had been inseparable and wanted to spend each and every day together. We also realized how much we loved those kids and both wanted to give them a stable and loving home.

It was a beautiful spring day in May and Jake and I were enjoying an ice cream while watching the kids play in Glover Park. With a big smile on his face, Jake looked over at me and asked me to marry him. I, without hesitation, said "yes." There I was, the woman who said she would never get married again, just said yes to sweetest, kindest and most loving man. It seemed it was the most natural thing in the world. I hoped we would get custody of the kids soon and we could all begin a new life together. I knew being a part-time mom was going a big change for me and a lifestyle I had never known. However, I had no idea my life was going to again take a 180 degree turn!

CHAPTER SIXTEEN

After placing the *Walk the Line* DVD on the floor with all of the other items I have collected, I felt a wry smirk forming on my face. It felt so good to love someone who loved and respected me for just plain ol' me. There was no pretending, no acting, and no illusions of a perfect existence. We laughed, cried, and supported one another without judgment. We were proud to let others know about our struggles and setbacks. Our hearts had both been so broken neither of us thought we would love again, but we were proven wrong. Our story started off with hardened hearts, but we both had grown to see love for what it was and what it can be. As I searched the bottom of the case for the few remaining items, I pulled out a signed, notarized, recorded official court order.

On a cold and windy Wednesday morning in November of 2007, I would officially become the mother of five year old twins. I thought initially I was taking on the role of step mom and felt I could handle that. I was a smart, loving, capable woman. I mean how hard can it really be? Boy, was I in for an enormous shock? When the Judge announced his custody decision, Jake was awarded full custody and reality began to sink in. I felt the color drain from my face, my heart palpitated, and I felt dizzy. These two precious children would be mine and Jake's responsibility 24 hours a day, 7 days a week for the rest of our lives. I was now a full-time mother at the age of 45. Once again I had to ask myself *what have you gotten yourself into.*

The original court order, issued in July of 2007, stated Andrea was allowed visit the kids every other weekend under the supervision of her parents. I knew that was going to be a goat rodeo. There was no way her mom and stepdad were going to enforce the rules set forth by the court. Andrea was ordered, per the final divorce decree, to move out of the marital residence and possession of the home was awarded to Jake and the kids. The Psychologist, who had been seeing Nat and Jakey from the beginning of this whole mess, felt they needed to return to what they knew as home for at least a year. This should give them a sense of stability and calm. I was not happy about moving into another woman's home, but knew that I had to suck it up and do what's best for the kids in the short term.

On a horribly hot summer day in August of 2007, Jake and I packed all of our belongings from my home in Marietta and moved into his marital residence. The residence was located in Cartersville, which is a small town about 45 minutes north of Atlanta. There are lots of "Leave it to Beaver" type neighborhoods and lots of old Victorian homes sitting regally upon manicured lawns. There was a church on every corner, and it took you an hour to get out of the grocery store when you went in for only a few items. Everyone knew who you were, and everyone knew your business. It reminded of my previous neighbors in Marietta, but the people in Cartersville were sincere and genuine.

Jake's marital home sat on an acre lot. It was a craftsman styled home and the rear of the home faced a scenic horse farm. The subdivision in which the home sat was called The Preserve. It was one of the sought after addresses in the city and when you told folks you lived in The Preserve, an eyebrow would usually raise. This neighborhood was not really my taste, but I knew once we got the kids settled, we would find a home of our own. The moving truck was fully loaded and off we went on our adventure. As we pulled into the driveway my new home, I had chills roll up my spine. I had no idea what to expect and what type memories remained in that place.

Upon arriving, Jake and I walked in the kitchen from the garage entrance. We looked around and quickly realized everything in the house was gone! Andrea had stripped the house bare. There was not even a crumb left on the kitchen counter. She did not leave the bedroom furniture, bedding, curtains, toys, or kid's clothes. All she left was two greeting cards Nat and Jakey had given their mom for her birthday, and lots of dirt and dust. I was thankful, at the time; the kids would be visiting their mom and grandparents this particular weekend. This would give Jake and I time to get things moved in. We wanted the kids to come home to a house full of furniture and not an empty shell. Our work was cut out for us. We had 48 hours to make this house into a home.

From Friday evening until Sunday afternoon, Jake and I worked our butts putting the house together. By the time the kids arrived on Sunday night, the pictures were hung, the furniture was in place, and I must say everything looked great. The kid's bedrooms were furnished and cute as could be. A wave of relief came over the two of us. When Nat and Jakey entered the house, they ran upstairs to their bedroom and I heard them both say "Wow, this was so cool!" *Whew,* I thought. We passed the first test. At that very moment, there was happiness and excitement I imagined had not been present in that home for a long time.

Over the next two months, visitation with Andrea continued and the kid's moods and temperament, when they returned each time, took a turn for the worse. Usually when the kids were dropped off, Papa Baker (Andrea's Stepfather) would park his car on the street in front of the house and let them out. They would run into the house and all hell would break loose. Jakey would start yelling and screaming as loud as he could, "You're a liar! I want to go and live with my mommy! You are evil!" This went on for months. The kids, while with their mom, were being coached again to say Jake abused them, but now I was in the mix too. As their visits continued, we knew something had to be done. As we observed the kid's erratic behavior, it became obvious Andrea's parents were not supervising her visit as ordered by the court.

This was no surprise to me. I knew when the court ordered this arrangement, it would not be followed. I also knew time would take care of that detail, and that time had arrived.

Jake proceeded to file paperwork with the court to review visitation. Since we had to wait a few months to get this matter on the court calendar, it was decided by all of the professionals to put Andrea's visitation on hold. It was clear the coaxing and coaching of these children had to stop. Enough was enough. Jake's attorney sent Papa Bart a certified letter notifying them that visitation was put on hold until the court could review the case. We had not heard from Andrea or her family after they received the letter. That was until a cold, damp Friday evening that October. It was about 7:00pm and it was getting dark outside. The kids were watching cartoons in the family room. I was in my bedroom surfing on my computer, and Jake was flying. The doorbell rang and the kids ran to the front door, looked out of the glass double doors, and shouted, "Miss Patty, it's a policeman!" Both had a fearful tone in their voice. The last time they saw law enforcement at their front door; they were removed by the State and put in foster care. The sight of a police officer scared them tremendously.

I opened the front door and officer introduced himself as Officer Root. He was with the Cartersville Police Department. The kids were standing on each side of me. As I looked out towards the driveway to the left of the house, I saw Andrea standing beside her dark green Ford Explorer. She stood there with her arms crossed with a defensive posture. Her mother, Louise was standing right beside her. The kids pass me calling out "Mommy, mommy, mommy!" Before I could stop them, they were already in the back seat of her car. I was petrified she was going to drive away with those kids and Jake and I would never see them again!

With a frantic tone in my voice, I pleaded with Officer Root to get the kids out of that car. He refused stating he was simply obeying a court order and I could not stop Andrea from seeing her children. I attempted to explain to him that we had requested a new court date in regards to visitation. The more adamant I was, the more enraged Officer Root became. He refused to listen to what I had to say. He informed me that if I did not allow the children to leave with their mother, he was going to lock me up. I told him that would be fine but these children were not leaving with this woman.

Officer Root got angrier, and I asked him if I could call Jake and let him know what was going on. Jake was on a trip to Arizona and I needed to speak with him desperately. Officer Root agreed to let me make that call. After talking with Jake about the events happening at the house, he proceeded to contact his attorney and explain the situation to him. Moments later, Jake's attorney, Tony Pancetta called our home and requested to speak with Officer Root. As Officer Root walked inside and answered the phone, I was hoping and praying Andrea would not drive off. She had been warned not to leave our driveway until this mess was straightened out. I hoped she would follow his instruction.

While on the phone with Mr. Pancetta, all I could hear was Officer Root saying "Yes sir, yes sir." I then overheard him saying, "I need to come in and see you. My wife has left me and will not let me see my son." It suddenly hit me. Officer Root was going through his own personal hell. I needed to cut him some slack. By the grace of God, Officer Root hung up the phone and told me he was leaving and hoped our situation was resolved soon. Under his breath, I heard him mumble, "There was no reason for a parent not to be able to see their child." I just let this go on by and acted as if I had not heard a thing. It was now time to go outside and help Officer Root get the kids out of the car, but he quickly asked me to stay on the front porch.

I stood there and watched Officer Root open the back door of the SUV and literally pull these kids out kicking and screaming. Andrea and her mom continued to stand beside the car, arms crossed, showing no emotion. There was such a commotion in our driveway several neighbors came out of their homes to see what was going on. It took several minutes to get both kids out of the car and back into the house. My heart was breaking watching these two little people having to be ripped from their mother's car. I was frustrated, angry, and perplexed. I kept asking myself over and over again: *Why had she done this? She knew visitation had been suspended until we returned to court. Why would she put them through this trauma? Haven't they already been through enough?*

Finally Officer Root, Andrea and her mom all left. It was all quiet on our street again with the exception of two hysterical and sobbing kids beside me. The poor things did not understand what had just happened. All they knew was the mean police man and Miss Patty would not let them go with their mom for a visit. These kids were traumatized and whimpering for their mother "mommy, mommy" pretty much all night long. I called the Chief Pilot at the airline, and let him know there was an emergency at home that required Jake. I needed him to come home as soon as he could. The Chief Pilot stated that would be fine and assured me Jake would be flying home within the next few hours. I needed him and the sooner the better.

October 5, 2007 was one of the longest nights of my life. The kids and I were having a nice, quiet evening at home and the next thing I know; there was a police officer at the door threatening to arrest me. I just do not understand why a parent would rather "torture" the other parent and wreak pure terror on their kids. Do they really hate the other parent more than they love their children? Was winning really all that important!

Andrea decided to drive into town, makes a big mess and then leaves me to clean up her destruction. That proves to me a mom does not have to give birth to a child to love, nurture, comfort, and care for them as if they came from her body. This night showed me just how much I loved Jakey and Nat and to what ends I would go to protect them and their fragile minds, emotions, and hearts. After 14 months of living in foster care, the kids were finally back in their home and about to start kindergarten. I had no idea how this school stuff worked. So I did what any other new mom would do, I went to the school and asked the school secretary.

A few days before school began; I went to the office at the Primary School. "So, what am I supposed to do now?" I asked the woman standing behind the desk. She was a very attractive, late thirty, blonde headed lady who looked at me and said "pardon me?" I repeated myself. She patiently asked me if I was talking about school starting or did I need help with some other matter. Her confusion sent me into a bit of a panic. Perhaps she thought I needed an immediate referral to a psychiatrist or maybe I just needed to be "committed" for observation. Once I settled down and my breathing returned back to normal, she began explaining the school schedule to me. She told me which bus the kids would be riding, what class the kids would be in, and most importantly, how the lunch schedule worked.

Relieved to have this information, I thanked the kind woman, and proceeded home with my head held high. Once home, I headed directly into my bedroom and had a mini meltdown. I kept thinking to myself: *I cannot do this. These kids need a mom who has a clue about what was going on in the world of parents. They don't need a 45 year old woman, who has no clue what to do, what to say, or how to handle the day to day responsibilities of parenting.* I cried for about an hour, pulled myself together, wiped my eyes, and wanted to kick myself in the butt for my self pity. I then went into the kitchen and started a delicious dinner of hot dogs and macaroni and cheese.

On first day of school, Jake was on a trip and it was up to me to get the kids up, dressed, backpacks filled with school supplies, fed breakfast and out the door. I somehow managed to do all of these things. Once they were out the door, I followed behind as Nat and Jakey ran to end of the driveway to catch the bus for the first time ever. I helped them get up the steps of the bus with their huge backpacks and introduced myself to the bus driver. I sighed as I watched this big yellow contraption head down the road. I walked slowly up the driveway and into the house. Passing by the mirror in the hallway, I looked up at myself and realized I still had on my pajamas. I had gone to the bus stop wearing boxer shorts! I was so frazzled trying to get everybody ready for their big day, I did not think about what I was wearing. Oh well, I thought: *I got done what needed to be done. As for fashion, tomorrow was another day.*

The first weeks of school went well and the kids were successfully settling into kindergarten. Nat and Jakey really liked their teachers and it looked as though the school year was going to be great.

The legal stuff was another story and wasn't over just yet. On a chilly morning, a few months after the kids started school, it was time to head back to court in our fight to get Judge Newton to permanently suspend Andrea's visitation. As 9:00am arrived, Jake and I were sitting in Judge Newton's courtroom waiting for Andrea and her parents to arrive and for Judge Newton to take the bench. We were also hoping the divorce would be finalized today. This mess had been going on for over two years and it was more than time to move on.

9:00am soon came and went with no sign of Andrea or her parents. About 9:30am, Judge Newton's assistant walked into the courtroom and handed Judge Newton a piece of paper. Apparently, Andrea had faxed a letter to the Judge's chambers stating she was not able to be in court today. The letter stated her mom was in the hospital with some sort of heart issues and could not travel. Of course, we were not happy at all with this, but Judge Newton had no choice but to continue the hearing until December. The only good thing to come out of the continuance was Andrea was not allowed to see the kids until all legal matters were resolved. Jake and I left the courthouse frustrated and disappointed and I have to say, our stress levels were soaring high. We decided we just needed to go and have lunch and a cocktail. That was exactly what we did. I was so ready to marry this man, but that was going to have to wait just a wee bit longer.

CHAPTER SEVENTEEN

I really don't know whether I should be happy or sad about the fact my suitcase is almost empty. There were so many memories locked away - many of which I chose to forget about until the unpacking began. I justified my "forgetfulness" because the memories were simply painful flashbacks of a time when all I could do was survive. Looking forward, I am sad and relieved that the truth and honesty I had come to know and accept will probably not be as "real" from this point on. Although, I am mindful that there will be times when I will slip back into a pattern of self sabotage. A pattern I have worked so very hard over the years to break.

Getting back to the business of unpacking, I find a beautiful, silver, engraved framed photo of a bride, groom, and two beautiful children. This picture makes me smile. The picture is of me, Jake, Nat and Jakey on our wedding day. The four of us are standing in a field of tall, green, swaying grass and the kids are looking up at Jake and I as we reach out and hold their hands. The wind was blowing and it felt as if angels were all around us. The picture is one of the most beautiful photographs I had ever seen

The morning of the wedding had been cloudy and gray, but after the ceremony, the heavens opened up and the light from above shone down on the four of us. This day was the beginning of my learning what true love, selflessness, and sacrifice was all about. On April 12, 2008, I woke up extremely early to prepare for what I knew was going to be an incredibly hectic day. I sat up in my bed and thought to myself "I am getting married in ten hours." I had sworn for years I would never get remarried and here I was staring at a buff colored wedding gown and veil.

A slight grin come over my lips and decided it was time to get up. I walked out of the bedroom and into the kitchen to make my morning coffee. Out of the blue a voice from the family room called out to me "Well, good morning bride." I jumped a bit out of surprise. I had completely forgotten that Jake's Aunts had come from South Dakota and Texarkana to attend the ceremony. I turned to my left and saw Aunt Margaret sitting on the sofa watching the morning news. I told her good morning in return and stood by the coffee pot hoping that watching it would make it brew just a wee bit faster. It didn't.

After five minutes, or so, I pulled the carafe out and poured myself a big cup of caffeine. The smell alone could almost make me do a back flip of joy but really did not think that would be a good idea seeing as though I will be walking down a long aisle in a few hours. I sat down beside Aunt Margaret and talked about Jake when he was a little boy and family stuff in general. There was a calm feeling in the air and I just had a good feeling today was going to be a truly memorable day. A few hours later, Katie, mom and I were off to the day spa for some pampering. We spent about 4 hours there before heading to the church to get dressed and have pictures made. I must say I really cherished the time I spent with my mom and sister. I am so fortunate to have them in my life to share special moments with. For them, I count my blessings.

The three of us arrived on time and headed to the bridal dressing room (which was also the church choir practice room). I put on my wedding dress and veil and stood in front of a full length mirror. I felt tears in the corner of my eyes. I felt so happy and loved that it was almost impossible to hold all of the contentment inside. This was a new sensation, and I liked it.

It was 4:45pm, and it was show time. I slowly walked down the stairs of the church with my mom holding my arm. It was comforting to feel her hand wrapped through my arm and just knowing she was beside me. She and I had been through such horrific times together it was nice to share the sweeter moments with her. While taking a step down each stair, we both talked about how we missed my brother and wished he was with us for this special occasion, but knew he had made the decision to withdraw from us.

Sadly, we had not seen Kris in over 8 years. It was a hard pill to swallow, but he was an adult and very capable of making his own decisions. His brain was pretty much fried from all of the drugs, but he could find either one of us if he really wanted to. I was of the opinion it was probably easier for him not to have to see me or my mom. When Kris looked at us, he was constantly reminded of the beatings, abuse, and torture we all endured. I really think he could not handle the constant reminders of those days.

As mom and I reached the bottom of the stairs, the grandparents, attendants, groomsmen, flower girl and ring bearer (Nat and Jakey) were all waiting to go into the church. I took my place, grabbed my step-dad's arm, and waited for my cue to walk down the aisle. I could hear Pachabel's Cannon playing and felt my heart swell with love. Once I got my bearings straight, I put my right foot in front of my left and next thing I know, the church doors opened. Standing in front of me were the people I loved, trusted and cherished most in this world. It was such a peaceful feeling to see true friends and family in that church wishing so much happiness for Jake and myself.

As I walked down the center aisle, I looked at the end of the lace runner and saw Jake. He had the biggest, sweetest smile I think I had ever seen. I could not get down that aisle fast enough and finally become his wife. The ceremony was over in the blink of an eye and down the aisle we walked as a married couple. I felt as though I was floating on air. It was such an incredible feeling knowing someone loves you unconditionally and only wants good things for you. For the first time, since attending vacation bible school as a young child, I felt safe, embraced and loved. The wedding party then proceeded out of the church sanctuary and stood in the vestibule to greet guests and have more pictures taken before heading to the reception.

As I stood waiting for more pictures to be taken, I felt a small tug at the bottom of my wedding gown and as I turned and looked to my right, I saw Jakey standing by my side. He had tears rolling down his tiny face. I asked, "Jakey, what's the matter? Why are you crying?" He looked up at me and said "Why does my daddy have two wives?" I guess I looked at him with a perplexed expression and he wailed," My daddy is married to my mommy and to you." As he cried harder, I tried to come up with an answer he could understand. But, was there really no answer that would sooth him and help him with this troubling question?

I bent down, looked him straight in the eye and told him daddy only has one wife and his mommy is not married to daddy anymore. I also explained to him she will always be his birth mom and love him. I let him know he would be living with me and dad and I was his step-mom. I also let him know I loved him more than he would ever know. He stopped crying and let go of my dress. "Where's the cake?" was his next question. I knew question time was done and we were moving on to the next phase of our lives.

The reception followed and it was so much fun. The food was delicious, the deejay kept the dance floor hopping, and a good time was had by all. Around 11:00pm the kids went home with our sitter and Jake and I went home. We could not believe it, we could finally share the same bedroom. We had been sleeping in opposite ends of the house as ordered in the divorce decree. I have to say it was not easy, but we honored the rules so there would not be any more drama...as far as the kids were concerned. The four of us could now "officially" live as a family and all of our last names would be the same. Both kids still called me Miss Patty and that was just fine. I was ready for normalcy and structure. I could start to see the light at the end of that dark tunnel.

After Jake and I got home from the reception, I took off my wedding gown, my veil and promptly put on a t-shirt and flannel boxer shorts. I had enough of this girly girl stuff and just needed to be comfy and that was exactly what I did. We would be leaving for Lake Tahoe early in the morning for our honeymoon. Ten minutes after changing into our pajamas, we literally "fell" into our bed and Jake began to snore. I tossed and turned and for some reason, my mind was racing so fast that I could not turn it off. I had things I needed to work through and it appeared tonight was going to be that night.

When Jake proposed to me a year or so ago, we both talked the wedding details and both decided that we wanted to be married in the church. As kids, we both went to church regularly and it was a very important part of our foundation as we grew up. However, when Jake became a teenager, he told his parents he did not want to go to church anymore. They told him they wished he would attend with the family, but were not going to force him to go. For me, church made up my social life and I loved going until I was sixteen. This was certainly not an option in my family, and we were told that we would go to church as long as we lived under my dad's roof.

I attended Beulah Baptist Church until I was eighteen years old. Beulah Baptist Church was a typical southern Baptist church. It had a white steeple, stained glass windows, huge double doors in the front, and a choir loft behind the pulpit. There was a separate building for our Sunday school classes, a fellowship hall in the basement of the Sunday school building, and concrete picnic tables behind the sanctuary. You could not have a Baptist church without outdoor tables for food on the grounds. It was my home away from home and will always hold a special place in my heart.

Once at college, however, I discovered freedom, beer, and fraternity parties. Church was not on my social agenda. I had such a jaded view of the whole organized religion thing by that time. My dad had been a Deacon, cried at the altar every Sunday, was known as a "fine, upstanding Christian man." Yet, he would go home after the church service and somebody would get beaten and/or verbally abused. I was of the opinion that if my dad was considered such a fine example of a Christian man, how could I trust anyone sitting around me in that sacred place? Were they all hypocrites? Now, for those of you still reading and thinking, I'm wrong for my views about church and religion, keep in mind this was my perception. A person's perception was their reality and my reality did not include attending church as an adult. The emotions attached the whole church experience were just too hard to overcome at this juncture of my life.

When married to Carr he informed me that he was an atheist and attending church was not an option. However, through all of the trials and heartaches in my marriage and divorce, I always felt something was missing in my life. It seemed like there was a hole in my heart I attempted to fill with a lot of different things. I tried using alcohol, money, work, and tennis, yet none of these gave me a long term sense of security, love or contentment.

When Jake and I started going to church together, I slowly began to realize I was feeling a sensation of love, acceptance, and commonality with the people in the congregation. I recognized the feeling but could not put my finger on where I had experienced it before. I lay in bed and looked at my television cabinet. I saw two teddy bears that I had purchased in London at Herrod's Department Store years ago. I began to put two and two together, Boom! It hit me like a shot between the eyes! The last time I truly felt these emotions was when I was in vacation bible school as a child! I remembered that I could not wait to go everyday and be with Ms. Agnes and Ms. Margo. They were always so happy to see me. They thought I was a precious child and talked about how Jesus loved me unconditionally. They told me he would never let me down, never hurt me, and he would never leave me. Both teachers would hug me and show me the love that I never received at home. It was love I so desperately needed. The realization came to me clearly and I knew what I needed to do: I needed to return to my foundation and let the love of God fill me with his spirit. This was the void in my life and no matter what I tried to fill it with, only God could make me whole.

On my wedding night, I got down on my knees and prayed. I asked God to forgive me for the years I turned away from him. I prayed he would continue to fill my soul with love and joy and help me to be good mom and wife. I prayed he would allow me to let go of the mistrust I had of people in church and I would allow them to love me.

I opened my eyes, tears were streaming down my face and a sense of peace came over me. I knew God had answered my prayers. It was time to get my act together and get myself right with God. I felt my eyes getting heavy but my heart was full. I looked over at my new husband and said just one more prayer. I thanked God for sending me this kind, loving, gentle man. I prayed that I show him the love he deserves. I wanted to love him, as well as, the kids with every inch of my heart and soul. I realized that night, without God, none of that would be possible. I am so thankful I saw all my blessings and was able to thank God for them.

CHAPTER EIGHTEEN

There are just two items left to be unpacked and I must say I am exhausted and numb. The simple task of taking things out of this old case has turned into a very introspective experience. I really like the person I am becoming. I am more confident, brave, outspoken, spiritually in touch, and willing to take the moments as they come even if it means flying by the seat of my pants. I did not ever think I would have the guts to stand up to my ex-husband since he knew how to push my buttons, but looking at the Order for Contempt papers lying here in this suitcase, I knew I did. I picked the papers up and held them up like a badge of courage.

It was 2008, and Jake and I had been married for only a few months. We had successfully gotten through his custody and divorce stuff, and both realized that it was time to deal with Carr. It seemed that dealing with our past had become a never ending battle. I had brushed a lot of stuff under the rug and put Carr on the back burner. It was now time to turn up the heat. When Carr and I divorced in 2004, He was ordered to put our marital residence on the market. I agreed to give him time to sell the property so he would not have to liquidate his 401K and take a huge tax hit. In the Marietta real estate market, a home such as ours would typically take up to a year or two to sell. I had received enough money in the divorce to get by for a while. I was assured by our real estate agent that the house should sell in 24 months at the absolute latest. I accepted this time frame since our realtor, Mr. Glover was one of the top agents in Marietta and his specialty was historic homes. I just sat back and waited for notification of when the house was under contract and the closing date.

I waited, waited, and waited some more. Every time I emailed Carr about the status of the home being sold, he wouldn't email me back. It wasn't until after two and a half years, it became crystal clear that something wasn't right. I was being left out of any discussions pertaining to our residence. I was afraid to keep emailing Carr since I knew he had an awful temper. I was trying not to rock the boat. But, enough was enough! I was going to meet with an attorney to see what could be done.

It was an amazingly muggy, hot, Wednesday afternoon in May and I walked down from the State Probation Office, where I was working, to Mr. Murdock's office. Mr. Murdock was my new attorney. He had been recommended by several friends and was known as a "good old boy local lawyer." His office was in a development comprised of single story buildings that had their own welcoming entrances. I opened the front door and was immediately standing in the reception area. The room was decorated in a traditional style with a mahogany desk, hardwood floors and a oriental rug lying under two tapestry chairs. A pretty young blonde walked out and asked me if I was Ms. Pacilli. I nervously told her I was and took a seat in one of the chairs to my right. She asked if I would like a soda or coffee and told that Mr. Murdock would be with me shortly.

As I sat in that waiting room, I felt my palms getting sweaty, my legs were shaking and I could feel that oh so familiar heat of my blood pressure rising. I couldn't believe I had to hire an attorney just to find out information about the sale of a home that was partially mine! Mr. Murdock came around the corner and introduced himself. He was about six feet tall, had gray hair, a ruddy complexion, and a southern accent that sounded like he had marbles in his mouth. He told me to come on back to his office and I promptly followed him to the back suite. When I first walked into his office, I noticed it was furnished with expensive furniture, draperies and artwork. Of course my first thought was, I cannot afford this man's services. I just wanted to run out, but I didn't.

Mr. Murdock and I began discussing my case. He started to become annoyed with the way Carr had been treating me and felt we could have him found in contempt of the original court order. The only sticking point was there had been no date put in the Settlement Agreement stating by what date the house had to be sold. I was not insistent on this detail since I had been assured by Mr. Glover that the house would have no problem selling within two years. I knew Carr didn't have the money he owed me just lying around. I took the high road thinking I could trust what I had been told. In hindsight, I had been duped. Mr. Murdock went over how the Motion for Contempt would be drafted. He said that Carr had not included me in the pricing and pertinent information in regards to the sale of our home. We discussed his legal fees and he was kind enough to give me a break. He said he respected the way I had handled myself in the Divorce and assured me his fees would be reasonable. I sighed with relief and was ready to move forward with my case.

Before I left Mr. Murdock's office, I decided I was going to muster up the courage to stand up for myself and fight. I had been a doormat for way too long. It was time to "hit the bully" figuratively speaking. I walked out of his office and wanted to sing and shout, at the top of my lungs, "I am Woman." I decided that probably was not a good idea since I was out in public and did not need any more rumors about me floating around Marietta.

Several weeks after my initial meeting with Mr. Murdock, I received an email from Carr. He stated, "He was doing the best he could to sell the house and could not believe I was taking him to court." The email upset me at first, and then I giggled. It was such a defining moment in my life. Carr no longer frightened me. Since my childhood, I had been a "whipping boy" for so many people. I had been physically, emotionally, and verbally battered by the people I was supposed to be able to trust. The people I should have been able to count on for love and support. I had cowered down for years out of fear. Whenever the abuse started, I mentally checked-out and let my mind go to a place serene and safe. I removed my soul from my body and took myself somewhere else. I referred to that as "survival mode."

The ability to detach was one of the best things I did to maintain my sanity. If I was been being screamed at or beaten, or both, I would go numb until it was over. I had struggled over the years trying to get the feeling back. Once you had experienced "shutting down," it was hard to emerge again. My walls had been stacked so tightly it will probably take the rest of my days to allow them to be torn down. I really want love, compassion and closeness in my life. I will pray and until the day the walls crumble, I will continue to struggle with attempting to find honesty and truth.

After several nasty emails from Carr trying to convince me not to go forward with the Contempt Action, the day finally arrived when we would meet in court. I was going to be face to face with the man who stomped on my self esteem day after day during our marriage. The man who told me, "I was nothing but a redneck and my family was white trash." The man who told me to "shut up" while we were in public places. The man who in a restaurant asked our waitress "to send over someone with a college degree so his order would be right." The man who embarrassed, humiliated, and tore me down, but did not break me.

I did everything to cover for him, make excuses for him, and smooth everything over so that I could have a little peace in my life. Since covering and making excuses was a natural part of whom I was, most of our friends and family didn't know the extremes of his behavior because I painted over the ugly stuff. Remember, I was a professional at this and that was probably one of the reasons people referred to Carr and I as "the perfect couple." I was an exceptionally good fabricator of the truth and everyone else benefited from this talent...but me.

I walked into the courtroom. I had Katie on my side, as well as, Mr. Murdock. I looked towards the defendants table and there he sat. That 5'6" man, with hair plugs and a familiar expression of hate on his face. He was so angry I thought he was going start ranting at any moment. He held it together somehow and we all took our respective places as the Judge took the bench. As Judge Stratford walked out from behind the wall with her black hair and black robe, she instructed us to be seated. She asked both attorneys if they were ready to present their cases and each said yes. As the proceedings got underway, Mr. Murdock called me to the witness stand. I stood up and could feel the daggers being shot in my direction. I kept reminding myself that he couldn't hurt me anymore. I silently prayed that God would send my special angel down to protect me and surround me with peace and grace. I sat in the witness chair for about thirty seconds. There was small nudge on my right shoulder and I suddenly knew that my angel was right there with me. I was going to be okay.

As Mr. Murdock asked me some general questions about my contact with Carr and Mr. Glover, he was showing that I had been left out of all pricing decisions being made in relation to the sale of the marital home. My testimony was cut and dried. Mr. Murdock sat down and Carr's overpriced attorney, Mr. Steele, got up and I dreaded this cross examination. Mr. Steele walked towards me. As I looked over at Carr, he had a cruel smirk on his face. Mr. Steele asked me if I had agreed not to put a date on the Settlement Agreement in which the home was to be sold. I told him I had agreed since I had been assured by Mr. Glover and Carr that I would be paid within 24 months. Mr. Steele then began asking fairly generic questions that really had nothing to do with why we were there. I figured since time billed was an attorney's bread and butter, Mr. Steele was buttering his bread on both sides. After about an hour on the stand, I was told I could step down. Hallelujah! I looked up and thanked "my" guardian angel for helping me get through this stressful time.

After I left the stand, Judge Stratford declared a ten minute break and left the bench. While all parties sat in the courtroom waiting for court to resume, I noticed commotion coming from the table where Carr was sitting. Carr was standing up and heading towards my table. As he approached, I could hear him yelling, "You don't deserve any money. You need to let all your friends and family know you now live on the wrong side of the tracks. You don't live on Cherokee Street anymore. You are just a piece of trash and will get nothing from me." As he continued his tirade, Mr. Murdock jumped up, stood toe to toe with Carr, and said "Boy, are you talking to my client? If so, you better sit down now. You are not in charge of this courtroom and better keep your mouth closed." Still surprised by Carr's actions, I jumped up from the table and headed to the restroom. As I opened the double doors leading out of the courtroom, I saw Carr. I was frightened. I didn't know what to expect. I began to walk faster towards the bathroom door and saw a figure out of my right eye. It was Mr. Murdock cutting Carr off at the bathroom door. I am not sure what was said but what I am sure of was that Carr went back to the defense table and did not utter another word.

Judge Stratford returned to the bench and Mr. Steele called Carr to the stand. As he sat in the witness stand, looking so docile and mild mannered, it was hard for me to believe he was able to hold it together. When Mr. Steele asked Carr about the sale of the home, Carr appeared to be choked up with emotion. He told the court how he was doing everything to get that home sold. He said he wanted nothing more than to pay me the money he owed me so we can both get on with our lives. His demeanor was so laid back and caring that I almost had to go to the bathroom and puke. I thought *"here we go again with another Academy Award performance."* Between Jay and Carr, I cannot believe neither of them ever came home with a gold statue.

After Carr's incredible performance, Mr. Steele said he was done with his witness and Mr. Murdock began his cross examination. He stood up slowly from his chair and walked with authority to the witness stand where Carr was perched. He started off asking him some simple questions about the divorce. As he continued questioning Carr, he started to get to the meat of the case. He asked him how he came about pricing the house, was I involved with the pricing decision, and when was the meeting held between me, Mr. Glover and himself to talk about the current price. Carr stumbled and told the court there wasn't a meeting. He said I had agreed on the price and he and Mr. Glover had kept me in the loop since the house was put on the market over 3 ½ years ago.

Engaging in bit of courtroom acting himself, Mr. Murdock looked Carr right in the eye and raised his voice an octave, "Let's face it Mr. Pacilli, you had no intention whatsoever of selling that house and paying Mrs. Hart the monies you owe her do you?" Mr. Steele jumped up and objected to the questioning. The judge over ruled. Carr worked on producing some tears and mumbled, "I am doing my best to sell the house and give her the money due to her." All Mr. Murdock could say was, "Sure you are." Carr stepped down from the stand and went back to the defense table. Judge Stratford advised the courtroom she had made her decision based on the evidence. She stated that she found Mr. Pacilli in willful contempt for not keeping Mrs. Hart in the loop and informed about such a large asset. She also found him in contempt for not including me in the pricing of the home. There were no attorney's fees awarded at that time, but I was thrilled. I knew it was a small victory, but it would set the stage for future litigation, if necessary.

It was December of 2008, and I was headed downtown to the Fox Theater, with mom, to see a Christmas show. My cell began ringing and as I answered it, I immediately heard Carr spewing off at the mouth. I asked him to calm down and tell me what was going on. He told me he had just fired Mr. Glover because he and his company, Harry Norman Realtors, were trying to steal money from him. I had absolutely no idea what he was talking about, but he told me that he was going to be interviewing for a new listing agent and he would get back with me when he narrowed it down. We could then both decide on a good choice. I thought about what he was saying for a minute and quite frankly was in support. It was probably time to get some new perspective on the sale of the home. Mr. Glover had the home listed for several years without any luck. I responded and told him that once he had a couple of good candidates to let me know and we could figure out which person would be best suited for the job. He thanked me and told me that he would get back with me soon.

About a month after Carr's phone call, I was driving past our house and there's a huge real estate sign in the front yard with the name Carla Hambrick on it. I was perplexed. I had no recollection of Carr calling me about Ms. Hambrick listing the home. I had heard her name in the community and knew she had a good reputation, but knew nothing else about her.For the next year, Ms. Hambrick had the listing and each month sent me a dinky marketing report that showed how many times the house had been viewed on the internet. This was not what I was supposed to get each month. I began thinking again that something wasn't right. I decided it was time to do some research on this chick. I Googled her name and could not believe my eyes:

The first thing that popped up on my Google search was a picture of Carr, Carla and her two daughters standing in "my" backyard getting ready for Carla's daughter's wedding. There were pictures of the reception near "my" reflecting pond and the reception was in "my" sunroom. I still considered the antebellum home mine since I was due a settlement from the proceeds. I was shocked, angry and just down right furious! The date on the photos read June 2007. I did the math and that Carr and Carla were dating when he hired her to list the house. According to the pictures posted on the internet, it seemed as though Carla had her family over for Christmas and Thanksgiving dinners, birthday parties and was using my asset for her event center.

There were also pictures of Carr and Carla at a Georgia Tech football game, in Las Vegas, and at a super bowl party. It was shocking enough to see the realtor that Carr hired partying away at the home she was supposed to be vigorously marketing and selling. But, seeing Carr fishing and at a super bowl party almost caused me to pee in my pants. Is this the same man that would not get near a pond or lake to fish because that was a "redneck" pastime or the man that thought football was ridiculous. The only sports that mattered to Carr were baseball and Formula One Racing. Oh Lawd! I almost fell in the floor in disgust and disbelief. Who was this man and did it just slip his mind to let me know that he was dating the realtor? Are you kidding me? Once I saw the pictures on the web, I did what any good ex-wife would do to preserve these memories - I copied the pictures to my hard drive. I printed them and put them in my legal file just in case I had to head back to court. From the pictures, it was apparent that Carla had no reason to want to sell the house since she was using it for her personal, entertaining pleasure. I sat and pondered this predicament for about an hour before deciding to send Carla a quick email. As any true southern woman, I wrote my email with a "bless your heart" tone. My email to Carla went something like this:

Dearest Carla,

I really enjoyed seeing your daughter's wedding and reception photos on Flickr.com. Everyone looked so beautiful, especially you and Carr. You may want to consider putting these in the marketing brochure that you had printed for the house. Just an idea.

As I hit the send button, I giggled and wondered what would happen next.

Within 24 hours of sending that email, Carla was no longer listing the home and Mr. Glover had the listing again. This was like real estate musical chairs and you know I had to send Carr an email commenting on the rehiring of Mr. Glover. About two days after I sent my charming correspondence, I received a note back from Carr stating that I was mistaken about Carla and that I had no basis for my accusations. He also added that in the spirit of cooperation, he had decided to let Mr. Glover list the home again. Wow, it was good to see that Carr was the man I had known and was as arrogant as ever. I could sleep that night knowing that I had one more victory under my belt and that my court file was getting thicker by the day.

My life became busier and crazier since getting remarried and becoming a full time mom to twins. There were many days I didn't know heads from tails. One day, I stopped briefly and realized that it was September 2010 and the house in Marietta still had not sold. I was also not being included in regards to pricing and marketing decisions. By this time, the market had gone to hell in a handbag. Carr still had the house way overpriced and there was no way that house would sell at that price. Jake and I talked about what our options were and decided it was time to take this mess back to court to see if we could put some pressure on Carr and Mr. Glover to get that home sold. A week or so later, I was sitting in Mr. Murdock's office. He was drafting a second Motion for Contempt. I really had no other option since the house has been on the market for over 6 years with absolutely no nibbles. I dreaded going back to battle with this man but knew it was the only way to get his attention and gain respect from Carr, Carla, Mr. Glover and most importantly, myself.

My court date was set for mid October and I was having a very hard time serving Carr with the court papers. It became obvious that he was dodging being served. I knew I was going to have to hire hire a professional process server to find Carr and get the job done. A friend gave me the name of John

Novatello. He was known as one of the best process servers in the area. After speaking with John, I posted on Facebook that I was at my wits end trying to find this goober and get him served. About two days after my Facebook post, I received an anonymous voice mail stating that Carr would be at a Sales Expo at the Georgia Aquarium the day after tomorrow. I could not believe my luck and immediately called John and gave him the details.

The day of the Expo had arrived. John informed me that he would call from the aquarium if he was able to get him served. Jake and I were having lunch around noon that day and as I was eating, I received a phone call from John. He told me there were hundreds of business men at this event and he was having a hard time finding Carr. I asked him to keep looking if he could and we agreed that he would search for about thirty more minutes. I went back to eating my lunch and my phone then started to buzz. I looked down at it again and realized it was John. I assumed he was calling back with no success. As I answered, I could hear John breathing hard. When I asked him if he was okay he said, "He has been served." I looked at Jake and yelled "The eagle has landed!" I then heard John telling me not to hang up. He had a great story to tell about the meeting.

John told me that he was about to give up getting Carr served when he decided to give it a couple more minutes. Before he started his second search, he needed to go to the restroom. While standing at the urinal, John said he looked over to his right and realized that Carr was standing right beside. John was a bit unnerved because he obviously was not planning on seeing the person he was to serve standing in the bathroom taking care of his business. John walked outside the restroom and waited for Carr to finish. As Carr walked out, John asked him, "Are you Carr Pacilli?" Carr looked at him thinking that he was a business partner and answered he was and extended his hand. John reached out and acted as if he was going to shake Carr' hand, but instead, he handed him the court documents and told him to consider himself served. John said that Carr turned white as a sheet and stood still looking angry and frustrated at the same time. Finally, we had gotten him served. I was so ready to get this over with and wanted so badly to move forward.

On Monday morning, Jake and I got up, got the kids off to school, and headed down to meet with Mr. Murdock to go over my case before court started at 1:00 pm. Shortly after we got to his office, he received a call stating that Carr's attorney was sick and could not make it to court today. I pitched an old fashioned hissy fit and told Mr. Murdock we were going to court and ask Judge Stratford for some help and that was what we did. Due to the length of time it had taken me to get Carr served and the game playing by his attorney, Judge Stratford special set a court date for the following Thursday. She stated that they better be at the hearing or there would be major consequences.

I realized that the ball was in my corner and all I had to do was ask for help. Why had I gone so many years and not turned to God? My foundation had been built on trust and love for the Lord, but through my trials, heartaches and abuse, I turned my back on what I knew. I returned to my knees and asked for forgiveness, mercy and strength to hold steadfast against my enemies. The day arrived to go to court. Although I had already been through this several times before, I still was hesitant and nervous. Mr. Murdock, Jake and I walked into that courtroom with heads high. Carr was seated at the table with his attorney. His girlfriend and ex-realtor, Carla was sitting outside of the courtroom with Mr. Glover. The two of them could not come in since they had been subpoenaed and would be testifying today. I took my seat at the all so familiar table. Judge Stratford walked out and took her place on the bench.

I was the first person called to the stand to testify since I had brought the action forward. Mr. Murdock skillfully asked basic questions to try and get me to relax. He asked me if I agreed to have Carla Hambrick list the house on Cherokee Street and I answered no. Carr hired her without my knowledge. He asked if Carr or Carla had disclosed that they were in a relationship when he hired her to list the house, and I said no. After this question, the judge asked me when and how I found out they were a couple. I pulled out the pictures I had downloaded from the internet. I asked her if she would like to see the picture of Carla's daughter's wedding, of Carla's family having Christmas and Thanksgiving dinner, or if she would like to see the picture of Carr and Carla standing in front of a Christmas tree all taken in my home. I handed the pictures to Judge Stratford and she looked through them and handed them back with a slight look of disgust on her face. Mr. Murdock said that he was finished with his questions.

Carr's attorney got up and waddled up to the witness stand to question me. She did everything to trip me up and get me angry. The purpose of this was to try and somehow make all of this look innocent on the part of her client. She talked in circles and asked ridiculous questions which proved to me that she really did not have a defense for her client, but she sure was going to get down in the dirt. I held my ground and finally the questioning was done. I was relieved, frustrated, and scared but I knew that God had promised me that he would not let me down. I had to hold on with all my might.

Carr got up to testify and pretty much acted like he had done nothing wrong and he was the victim. He told the court that I was aware of his relationship with Carla and was fine with it. He then testified that he never fired Mr. Glover, but that he felt that it had been time for a change. He said that Carla was the perfect person to fit that bill. Carr pulled out his victim card and started with all of the excuses as to why the house had not sold. He talked about the market being bad, his financial woes, and just went on and on. Of course, he didn't address the fact that the house was extremely overpriced and the appearance of the home was not equivalent to the price being asked.

Carr, Carla and Mr. Glover all finished their testimony and all three of them had major memory failures and just could not remember all of the details and events leading up to this day. This lends a whole new meaning to selective memory. Once everyone finished presenting their cases, Judge Stratford told the court that she has once again found Mr. Pacilli to be in willful contempt. He had hired Carla Hambrick, his girlfriend, and did not disclose their relationship. Also, she went on the state that since I did not know all of the relative information to make an informed decision about the change in realtors, the agreement that we supposedly made was not valid.

Judge Stratford continued to go over her ruling and when she got to the part where Carr had to pay my attorney's fees, I thought his head was going to blow off. He started rocking back and forth and I could tell he was urging his attorney to do something about the decision. I looked over at Mr. Murdock and he whispered to me, "Let's get out of here now." Jake and I got up from our seats and headed for the door. As we walked by Carla, who was sitting in the back of the courtroom, she looked up at me while chomping on her chewing gum and shot evil looks at the three of us. We keep on walking and did not look back.

We walked to Mr. Murdock's office and all three of us had a seat. I think I was in a state of shock. Judge Stratford listened to me, respected me, and did the right thing on my behalf. The feeling was so new and strange, but was very uplifting and confirming. Jake and I thanked Mr. Murdock and headed out for some dinner and a celebratory drink. At that moment, all was right with the world. I was feeling so good and had a new confidence and liked the taste of victory. Nevertheless, the air in my tires was about to deflate.

Three weeks had passed since my court date and all was quiet until today. I checked my email as I did several times a day and noticed I had new mail. I opened it and saw it was a Motion for a New Trial. Carr's attorney had also filed a Notice of Appeal. Was this man really so vindictive that he would spend thousands of dollars appealing a ruling that required him to pay attorney's fees of $2,800.00? I knew the answer. As Katie had said, "Carr would go to his deathbed doing everything in his power not to pay you and therefore in his mind, winning." Unfortunately, I had to agree with her.

I contacted my attorney and asked what we were to do now. Mr. Murdock told me the hearing date was set for October 31st, and all we had to do was show up and see what Judge Stratford decides. I was told that it is almost impossible to have a judge overturn their decision, but we could only wait and see. I wish I could tell you what the outcome of the appeal was, but unfortunately, it will happen after my story has been told. What I can tell you is that I will not be a victim and I will stand up for myself until the battle is over. One way or another.

CHAPTER NINETEEN

Well, dear friends, the time has come to unpack the last article in my suitcase of secrets. The terror and trauma I experienced in my life and, I'm now sharing, has led me to triumph. By reliving the past, marked by pain, abandonment, sorrow and extreme disappointment, I am able to peacefully put these memories to rest.

I'm sitting cross-legged on my bedroom floor and looking at this large pile of memories. It is late afternoon and I have opened my wooden shutters so that the soft light of dusk can surround me. Jake has taken the kids fishing at one of their favorite spots, and I am here alone with my thoughts and memories. It seems that over and over again, history has repeated itself until, at the age of 49, I had broken the cycle of "being a victim."

As a young child, I was convinced that I was not worthy of love and acceptance. As an adult, I was still being told that I was not good enough, smart enough, or pretty enough to deserve love. Putting up walls and packing things away was my only protection. I stacked concrete blocks around my heart. I was bound, bent and determined not to let anyone penetrate these barriers.

It was a sunny day in August of 2007, when the concrete walls finally gave way. It was a Saturday morning around 11:00am. I was sitting in a lounge chair under a huge oak tree in our back yard. Jake and Jakey were not home. They had gone to a Cub Scout litter pick up at Dellinger Park. As I sat and read my Southern Living Magazine, Nat swam up to pool steps in front of me and said "Mom, my heart smiles when you smile." Her small face with beaming and I could feel that these words came straight from her heart. These "sweet and precious" words of love shook me to my core. There was no agenda to this comment, just an open, innocent heart. As the next several years passed, the love shown to me by my children, my husband, and my God was immeasurable. Returning to my faith opened my heart and filled the void that for so long lived deep inside of me.

My friends who are reading this and can relate to what I'm sharing, I must caution you that should you embark on a journey to healing, it will not be an easy one. You will step forward and then step back. You will have good days and bad days. Surround yourself with loving, caring, positive people that will lift you up, even on the worst days. The trauma you have been through is a part of who you are. You can either embrace it, or you can let it control your future. The decision is up to you. Most of all, when the days get cloudy and gray, fall on your knees and pray for peace, guidance and understanding. Know that everything happens in God's time and he is the keeper of the clock.

The final words written on these pages will consist of raw, sometimes awful and sometimes comical events that have made me who I am today. Please know that for the first time in my life, I am strong enough to share these journal entries, to laugh and cry, and then put them away for good. These entries are the events that have led me to this place, and I am so thankful that I survived and can now share some of them with you.

August 1972 ~ We had just moved to Douglasville and I hate it. I don't know anybody here and have no friends. Last night, I said at the dinner table that I want to move back to Atlanta and get away from the stupid place. My dad got up from his chair at the end of the table, walked over to me and grabbed me by my arm. He drug me down the hallway to my room and hit me on the back and legs until I said I was sorry. He dropped me on the bed and told me that "I better be glad that someone wanted me and be happy for all that he has done for this pathetic family." I hate this man and wish that my momma would take us and move somewhere new. My back and legs are hurting so bad right now. I hope mom comes to my room and sneaks me in some aspirin. I am hungry too but I better be quiet and go to sleep or he will be back.

November 1973 ~ Mom is in the hospital having some kind of operation and I am here with my sister, dad, and brother. Tonight, I was lying on the couch in the den and was watching TV. My dad came in and sat down on the floor. He put his hand under my blanket and started touching y private parts. I got so scared and almost threw up. He keeps touching me and then leaned up and whispered in my ear "if you tell anybody what happened here, I will kill you, your mom and your brother. Do you understand?" I nodded my head and went to my room. This man beats me and my brother, and now he is touching my privates. Why is this happening to me and why do I have to go to school and church and lie about this man? I hate my life.

October 1975 ~ I had my first visit to the female doctor today. It was just awful. Mom took me because I had lost so much weight in the last year and my period has stopped. She has no idea that my dad is touching me and I had decided to stop eating. The doctor made me get on a table with just a paper thingy on, and then put some cold metal things inside of me. It was disgusting. He told my mom that everything looked fine and that it was probably just a hormonal thing and not to worry. I was so hoping that he saw something that would tell my mom that something was wrong, but I was not so lucky. Dad was waiting at the kitchen door when we got back and looked at me with those evil brown eyes and asked me if everything was okay. I told him the doctor said everything was normal. I am now in my room writing this and hoping that he will stop this gross, sick behavior. Please!

September 1976 ~ It is Sunday afternoon and we had just gotten home from church and had lunch. Church was good but I had to watch the "monster" do his whole church routine again today. When the pastor called for folks to come down and pray at the altar, my dad was the first one to go. He bent down on one knee and began sobbing and whaling like a freak. Several men in the church went down and put their hands on his shoulder for support and there was not a dry eye in that place. After the church service, all these church members came up to our family as we were walking out and told us how lucky we were to have such a God fearing, decent man for a father. I nodded my head and walked towards the car mumbling to myself. "Yeah he is a great guy. He beats, molests, demeans, and tortures me, but I guess if you think that is what a Christian does than more power to you." I was starting to distance myself from the church in small ways. Each Sunday, I would sit and look around and wonder so who in here is living a lie like my family. I can't trust anybody.

January 1977 ~ It is my 15th birthday and in a couple of hours, a few friends are gonna come pick me up and we are going to go down to the Omni and go ice skating. I was excited and could not wait to go. Before I got dressed, I was sitting in the den watching TV. Katie decided to get in front of the television and do some cheers. I told her to move, over and over again, but she would not. I got up and pushed her away from the TV. When I pushed her, she tumbled over and hit her forehead on the arm of the sofa. She wasn't hurt, but as she fell, my dad came into the room and thought that I had thrown her into the couch. His face was red, eyes glazed, and he came over to me, grabbed me by the neck, and shoved me into the sliding glass door in the room. I hit that door so hard that I fell to the ground. I reached up and touched my head and saw blood on my hand. I was crying so hard that I could hardly catch my breath. He looked down at me and said "shut up now. You better not ever lay a hand on your sister again. You are nothing but a fat cow and you could hurt her. You get in your room and call your loser friends and tell them that you are not going anywhere." I pleaded with him to let me go. It was my birthday, please. He just laughed and told me that he could care less what day it was. I was a pitiful piece of crap and they probably did not really want me to go anyway. So, I called everybody and made up a lie about why I couldn't go. I crawled in my bed and spent my birthday alone with a lump on head that hurt like hell. I had no cake, friends, or hope on my special day.

February 1988 ~ Carr is leaving for a trip tomorrow and I really don't want him to go. I'm going through a bad time and just need him to be here. He told me that he has to go if he is going to have to support me. I went and got myself a beer from the fridge, then another and was sitting in our bedroom crying and having a "moment." I am not sure what brought this about but I had made an observation about myself. I had a lot of really good days, but have some dark days too. This stuff that I had shoved down so deep that it is buried in my soul, is triggered sometimes by music, a movie, or sometimes it just creeps up a little and haunts me. I cant quite put my finger on what is causing this anxiety today. As I laid on my bed with my head buried deep in my pillow just sobbing, Carr comes in the room and pulls me by the shoulder so that I was looking at him and said "sometimes I wished I had never married you." Those 8 words were so piercing that I will never forget them. We had only been married for two months and this is how my new husband feels. More disappointment. Why cannot I just be loved?

March 2000 ~ When Carr and I got married, we both were convinced that we did not want children. With what I had been through as a little girl, how could I ever be a good mother? Carr did not want children because he said that he did not want to give up his grown up toys for a baby. I remember my mom saying to me when I was about 13 year old, "You are too selfish to ever a child." These words have stayed with me for all of these years and have played over and over. As I hear this tape repeating in my brain, I think I really started to believe that I could not be a good mom. It is a cool, crisp Saturday morning in March and I had a funny feeling both physically and mentally. I think I am pregnant. Even though sex was not really a part of my marriage, for the last 5 or so years, Carr and I did have a moment around Christmas last year. I guess maybe we were feeling the Christmas spirit and next thing ya know, I may be having a baby. We did not use any protection since I had major surgery years ago and was told that it would be virtually impossible for me to conceive. So, I am going to the drugstore to get a pregnancy test. I did not mention a word of this to Carr because I knew that, if by some ity bity chance that I am pregnant, that he will blow a gasket. And if I am not, why cause a scene when it is not necessary. I drove up to the Eckerd Drugs across from Kennestone Hospital and got a 99% accurate type of test. I went home and 20 minutes later, I looked down and there was a plus on the test. What, oh my gosh, I am pregnant. So I went back to the store and got another test and took it. It was positive also. How am I going to tell Carr? He is going to be so mad? I am gonna be a mommy. I went to my bedroom for about an hour trying to figure out the right words to say. I guess I needed to just come right out and tell him that I was pregnant and I am happy about it. So I walked down those old, creaky, stairs and asked Carr to come out of his office. As he walked towards me looking annoyed, I just came right out and said "I am pregnant." He stood there looking at me with a look of pure hate on his face. He was furious. He told me that he was not happy about this and that if I thought, I was going to have this baby, he was going to leave me and the baby penniless. He stormed out of the room and I sat in the floor cried. What am I supposed to do now? I am so afraid that the stress, along with my medical issues, will cause me to miscarry. Two months later, my worst fears came true, baby lost. After the loss of my baby, I lay in our guest bedroom and refused to sleep in my bed. I could feel hate and rage for the man I had married. I fell asleep around 8:00pm that night and when I awoke the next morning Carr was gone. When I called him on his cell, he informed me that he was on a trip. This man who I should have been able to depend on in good times and bad, left me in that big house, by myself to grieve the loss of my baby. I am starting to loathe him more and more each and every day. Maybe it is not meant to be for me to be loved. Maybe I am just unlovable. I tried to be the best person I could be, but all I get in return is people that are suppose to love me stomping on my heart. The pain was so sharp, in a physical and emotional way.

July 2007 ~ I am now a full time mother to 5 year old twins. These two little people depend on me for pretty much everything. I have to say that this was a whole new lifestyle for me and I had to get used to my new surroundings. I have to adjust to, when taking a shower, having 4 little eyes looking up at me and talking nonstop. I have to adjust to my son coming into the bathroom while I am taking a bubble bath and pointing to my breasts and asking "do those things float?" I have to learn how not to freak out when I get into the bed and there are plastic spiders, frogs and snakes under my covers. And I really had to work on not getting nauseous at all the stuff that comes out of those little people such as snot, poop, puke and other non-descriptive particles that they leave on the furniture, the car seats, and on me. The more I am around these funny, entertaining and precious kids, the more I let them into my heart. I am beginning to feel the power of a mother's love. I may not have given birth to these twins, but I can tell you that the love that these children give me is one of the greatest gifts I have ever been given.

As I come to the end of these life changing pages, there is one important thing I would like for you to embrace. When times are dark and you are feeling hopeless, reach out and help someone else. The greatest gift you have is to show compassion to others. When you show kindness, you will find that it's you that ultimately receives the gift. If you remember only one thing I have to share, let it be: Love yourself and love others.